FREDERIC LEON

"I used to want to change the world, but now I just want to leave the
room with a little bit of dignity."

Lotus Weinstock

ANTHONY DWIGHT PEEBLES

Written by Anthony Dwight Peebles

Edited by Jeri Frederickson, Joel Martinez, and Kristin Sgroi

Cover photo/design by Khalil Anthony for

URBANFOLK BOOKS

drink_ #1

INT.: Mid-day. Greyhound bus departs Los Angeles filled to capacity
with stories, one-way tickets, and sullenness. Some of the stories
leaving Los Angeles are myths and fables, others unedited and raw
autobiographical accounts. Only the respective authors, accompanied
by the tales, know which are which. One story along with its author
looks out onto US interstate 5 and counts the dreams in disrepair.
Destination: San Francisco. It's too hot to be this late. He, Fredric, the
author, looks up at the moon, hoping for cool rays. Isn't that what the
moon is: the antithesis of the sun? An 11:15 p.m. departure and about
as many drops of alcohol and tears—1,115.

*

Packed bus, swanky NY nightclub, no short skirts or
alcohol here - at least not for sale. Plenty of sweat, body
heat, and a limited amount of fresh air. There is not even
enough space to walk, not to mention space to dance. Only
this smell that my body has taken on as its own. Since I'm
not accustomed to it (the smell) I make snide remarks about
myself to the passenger riding beside me. We both laugh.
Some amalgamation of all the smells trapped inside this
cheap mass transportation device has taken over my

armpits - and the heat from the packed bus is literally cooking the odor into my skin.

Riding the Greyhound bus always seems to be a study, a microcosm of our socioeconomic issues in motion. Everyone talks about the middle-class and the rich, but what about the "real" America? Riding always makes me reflect on what I appreciate most about my life, choice. (At least the façade of choice.) Each time, an intense face-to-face encounter with the world that we really live in, instead of dealing with my circumstances, I immediately avoid looking inward and stare at the folks in the bus.

Poor brown and poor black people, poor white people, basically poor people, all the same. What about poor Asians? Poor Asians? These sad and contented faces, increasingly questioning my own existence and economic status. The Greyhound reeks of class issues and socioeconomic nightmares deeming this transportation device necessary, affordable, and the poor person's only choice.

Scattered plastic-bag-luggage-motion. Just being among the masses in this "court appearance" or "DMV" kind-of-way always makes me feel bad about the world in general. I should stop riding the Greyhound but I can't because sometimes I don't have the money for anything else. Even though my shoes cost three times the amount of my ticket.

I decided to relocate back to San Francisco after leaving the city of drugs, wonder, and bridges - for LA just eight months ago. I moved to LA to finally see what it was like to live together with someone. *That someone being my man.* I was in a relationship with what I thought to be a beautiful man. A beautiful man who loved me and who I thought I genuinely loved. The only problem with the plan was the "beautiful one" did not want to be with me anymore, i.e., smashing the picture, always, every time. Fucking prince songs.

So the move, and smoggy-ass Los Angeles don't hold any special meaning for me anymore. I still love the smog and all but I have no one to enjoy those beautiful "nuclear" sunsets with, you know? So I bought a one-way ticket and boarded this stink soup.

I just can't see myself in Los Angeles without the man I moved there to be with. I can't see myself at all come to think of it. All I see is the man I love and all I did was waste time with him and the "fucked-up" reality that he knew he did not want this to work out. The truth of the matter is he invited me to "la la" land to break up with me. Mutha-fucka!

My life feels contrived, some sort of lie that I agree upon and live out as if he is the puppeteer and I am the marionette puppet. Sometimes I can still feel the strings being pulled, and my lifeless, limbless existence moving on down the road. The WIZ is a bad mutha-fucka if you believe in all that lights, camera, and action mess. As if the character in this motion picture that gets dumped and left alone in a big city, selling himself in order to eat each day, turns out to be me. I mean sans prostitution and starvation, but I used to love him.

However fucked up that love was; I believed in it. I took care of it like a lioness takes care of her cubs, or a drug addict takes care of his habit – to the teeth, and at all cost. I caressed and matured it. Made my daily bread from it. Sat at the head of the table and prayed for it. And for it to end as soon as my feet stepped off the plane and onto Los

Angeles soil was beyond my imagination and my control. Mutha-fucka!

I thought I was in control of this relationship. I thought I was in control. It made sense to me. Before this relationship there was actual control, at least over my own feelings and myself. I lived by this love. I mean I was not one of those dumb blonde chicks who pretend that everything is okay when it's not. (I know that was a cheap shot on blonde chicks, but hey I'm human. I'm sure you got a few jokes about a black bi-sexual guy getting dumped once he gets to LA.) I knew we had our issues, but we were working those out, at least that's what I thought.

When we met, I was not seeing men, at least not actively nor consciously. Between us, the term/acronym/ and "fucked-up" media sound bite, the "DL: down low" was foreign to every man I may have crossed the line with prior to the world-wide witch hunt of men who fucked men, and fucked women, but didn't tell everyone about it.

It was obvious to me that I had feelings for men that could not be met through the immediate bonding of sport stats, misogynistic barber shop talk, and homophobic diatribes among the "fellas". You know after a lot of drinks, late at night, when we're drunk, and your hand has been on my left thigh for ten minutes while you talk shit, yea, that and then.

I knew I wanted more from men. I never knew what I wanted till I met William.

My name is Frederic.

I lived in LA for eight long - gas guzzling, short - coffee sipping, lonely (hearts club) months alone. And it was good and bad. Funny how good and bad hang out together when you concentrate on the binary as the sole reality for your emotional content. But with all things a time comes when you need to pack up your shit, change your address, and leave.

I decided to leave the city of lost angels before I became one. There is something insidious and ironic about moving somewhere to be with someone, having huge, gigantic, and what would seem impenetrable reservations at first, but then opening up and taking the leap anyway. Only to have the person holding the safety net, i.e., (my lover), not only move the net so that you, ("I"), fall, (fell), on your, (my), face; but to have said "lover" leave the country in the process – Ouch!

I endured the pain of landing face-first on the hard concrete and found a beautiful place to live. I moved into a huge flat in the Silver lake area of Los Angeles. It seemed to be one of the only areas where people could live without a car. I am a fan of cafes, and shops, and people milling about, which is the direct opposite of the reality of Los Angeles. Unless of course you drive to a neighborhood to pretend that you were just walking around. In LA, we drive two blocks to get cerveza and possibly forty-five minutes one-way for marijuana. It was frightening at first to realize that without a car I might not be able to get any beers, or cigarettes, but then I realized the block and a half walk would not kill me. Anyway, I had scored when it came to places to live without a car, and alone. If any of this could be considered scoring.

I needed a space that would be able to hold all of me, be able to allow my edges to smooth out. An apartment where I could cry and sleep, eat and possibly fuck, but definitely not think of William. Felt like I needed something to replace this huge hole inside of my rib cage, where my heart used to reside. I painted all the walls different colors and bought reused furniture to decorate my new home. I, humpty dumpty, putting the pieces together again. Post-Having-a-Great-Fall-Trauma.

I began painting and writing again. Ever since I was young, painting and writing saved my mind from what I considered impending doom of adulthood. I held onto the little pieces of my life that felt like they were unraveling and made art with them. Sometimes, it was a remedy for the long nights alone without my mother; I would sit alone while she was at work, or at school, painting and writing until there were no naked sheets of paper left. That is when I started to paint and write on the walls, which by the way my mother hated, but for some reason allowed me to continue to do. She said I was her little Egyptian Pharaoh who had forgot that writing on the walls had been replaced with words on papyrus.

It has been a while since I've painted, or written for that matter. I refuse to paint. I refuse to write. William always **adored** my work and I do not want to **like** anything he **enjoyed**, especially anything he **adored**. I used to **adore**

William. I want him to *erase* from my life now like when you *erase* a contact in your cell phone - *swoosh, erased, gone MuthafuckA...*

i spent my days mixing paint. mixing up new ways of thinking. attempting/hoping not to lose my mind. change the color of my situation through the different colors on my palette. (that would be nice.) long days-nights alone. reading books that i had read twice, looking through old photos, cutting out william's face and replacing his face with mine. nostalgic haze. refusal of the present kept me warm at night. each thought racing back and forth in the beautiful home and the wonderful strides writing and painting, then the record would scratch and i would begin to think of William; i would begin to think of william, of william, of wiliam. my relationship with him...

end.

and this time i would have to trust the universe enough not to go back. Please, buddha, help me not go back. but, how do you go back to someone who left you? maybe that was the frustration, the constant dilemma regarding my ex, the fact that he left me this time. swirling like colors mixing, tips of paintbrushes slightly rushing colors against white canvas. the idea that the day would come when mixing paint would only make me think of just mixing paint and not of william thrilled the shit out of me.

All of that to say I've decided to leave Los Angeles and go back to San Francisco. Leave William to come back to myself, so to speak.

The bus's tires rotate not unlike the enchanting iron spoon in a witch's cauldron, spinning round and round, reaching and extending, pulling and prodding – calling forth all promises of a change in scenario, a change in me. All in an attempt to grab hold of my imagination, spinning ferociously, at times out of control. Like those tires, my dreams, thoughts and ideas begin leading my heart again. Reminding me of the famous quote by Willie Wonka: "we are the music makers and the dreamers of dream." I dream again, making music, seeing colors splashed against the night's sky and feeling the brightness of the moon against my cheek, like the sun's warmth on the winds' breath. I dream. And it is good.

Awakening, now, I found myself and the other storytellers

in Bakersfield, and I think on all the cigarettes I smoked today. I like cigarettes. A lot of what is contributing to the smell we create on the bus is stale cigarette smoke. I light another Marlboro and think of what lies ahead. A cigarette, like an old friend's kiss, who has shit breath. I always wondered how anyone could kiss someone who smokes if they don't smoke themselves - now that must be love.

Four more hours on the bus pass and a train ride to a friend's house where I will crash for a couple of days. When I first moved to SF, I thought sleeping on someone else's floor or couch was beneath me. It was crass, weird, and absurd. 'I ain't sleeping on nobody's floor or funky ass couch.' But when I realized how expensive hotels and even hostels were in that town, and how hard it was to find an apartment, and the fact my temp agency check was always late...I had to suck up my pride and roll up the last two bucks I had to my name and stick them back in my pocket and deal with my "temporal" homelessness - by any means necessary.

The bus moves tranquilly and serenely like caterpillars on a dry leaf slinking and winding their way back home. We slowly approach the San Francisco bus terminal, and I feel myself graduating from larva to black-winged butterfly as the city's lights enrapture my metamorphosis. The doors open, and the musk disembarks the bus before the first passenger escapes. Like a sultry blues singer's voice, dark and dense, creeping through the crowd touching that space in her heart where pain resides. We exit; slow molasses, as the keys twinkle away the early morning dew.

----

sf: moving.

7:15 a.m. I arrived at my friend Jon's pad at around seven fifteen in the morning and take a shower. He left the keys for me under his doormat. I rushed to get to the gym.

7:56 a.m. 24 hr. Fitness Center: As I moved from the treadmill to the barbells, I began mentally working out the remainder of my day. I remarked to myself as I showered that I had started feeling like my old self again. I always laughed at the notion of feeling like our "old selves again". Like what and who were we feeling like when we weren't feeling like ourselves in the first place? As if, 'I felt like Catherine Zeta-Jones this morning, and I couldn't bare myself!' Or something awfully scary like that. Don't get me wrong, I know the value of coming back home when we have been gone too long, but the problem with the adventure away is that sometimes you just can't go home.

10:03 a.m. I made a phone call to my new employer and agreed to meet up with him at four o'clock. One of the exciting aspects to this move was the promise of a new job. My life is a jigsaw puzzle, and I connect each moment to the next with an intention of bridging dots; but when dots don't connect there is disorder; so Connect Four is not just a game to me.

Conjunction junction how's that function?
I got three favorite cars that get most of my job done.

I've always looked at that game in reference to my life as if I am aligning the four directions of myself when I am deciding what my next move in the game of life is going be. When it's good, it's great… and when it's bad, there is seldom a connection.

11:02 a.m. My body was exhausted, but the excitement had kicked into overdrive, and I knew that something great was incubating inside. I decided to get a bite to eat, Mexican food, in the Mission district. This used to be one of my favorite past times, sitting under the sun in the Mission district, eating a taco, and drinking a Jarritos soda.

I sit in the sun for an extra minute thinking of LA. The sun feels the same, but I feel changed, different.

3:45 p.m. I get off the 7 Haight bus in the midst of a beautiful flow of people coloring the streets. It doesn't matter what time of day you go to the Haight-Ashbury district of San Francisco, you will always feel as if you are walking through a parade. Each person walking past holds something special for me, I think. I smile, and a few people smile back. There seems to be a sense of anticipation in my stomach as I walk down the busy street toward this next opportunity. These colors make me think of paint. Dripping on my shoes, splashing, crashing against the white canvas, again there is color and movement.

I entered the colorful entrance.
A mural of Malcolm X, Cesar Chavez, Dolores Huerta, MAO, Jack Kerouac, and James Baldwin was being painted at the school's entrance.

When I reached the third floor, empty desks, moving boxes, old couches and rolling blackboards were cluttered throughout. My eyes darted back and forth across those artifacts of education. These tools we use to educate, spiraling out of classrooms, empty computer boxes occupy tops of shelves and corners of cluttered rooms.

I walk down the hallway, looking into each classroom visualizing little brown hands raised in excitement, possessing the answer to the teacher's questions, attentive and active in their educational careers. I listen closely and hear gossip and laughter from the imaginary middle school students who will fill these desks in a few weeks. I begin to smile again and laughter streams from my eyes. I laugh out loud and continue walking. This maze is needed; unrelenting symbols of what I am walking into are forced into my conscience-ness, and I am made present to this new existence.

Frederic = 6th grade Humanities Middle School Teacher?

I finally make it to the Principal's office. A smiley-faced gentleman, white, maybe forty-three years old, offers me a handshake and the warmest eyes I've ever seen as I enter his amazingly organized office. His powder blue tie loose around the neck, two buttons undone on his starched green button-up shirt grab my attention early on. His Dockers slacks fit snug around the waist, as if he needs to lose some weight. He also wears loafers with dimes in them. Actual dimes. 20 cents.

There are moments when we know we are in the right place and having ideals isn't really that bad of an idea. I hadn't seen loafers with dimes in them since the late 80's.

"So, we are happy to have you here Frederic," he said, with that same smile. "I know we asked a lot of you to move here in one week. We need you here. The students need someone like you here advocating for them. After your interview last week, I knew that you were the right one for the job. Someone with a heart and sense of the world that we live is what we need at this school. You know this is a new school, and a small school at that, we have worked hard making sure the students are our main concern. Oh, here ya go, if you wouldn't mind filling out these papers?" His hands had been moving so fast that I could barely concentrate on his words. It kind of freaked me out when he handed me the papers that he wanted me to sign. I grabbed hold of them and continued to ~~watch his hands move~~, listen to him speak.

"blah blah blah blah blah blah blah blah blah blah blah blah blah"

Flashes of students running in the hallway blur in and out as he speaks. I wipe my eyes and try and focus on filling out the papers in front of me.

I snap out of the dream. Open my eyes.
"I am excited to be here," I say and look up at him.

"Again, thanks for accepting the job on such short notice. I know you are looking for a place to live and all, (pause) ...so for the time being, if you would like, you can stay in my one bedroom apartment. My wife and I split once, and I kept it for the rough times, ya know? Just renting it out while things are good. That's another story in itself. It'll be available on Monday, if that's okay?" He hands some more paperwork to fill out.

Alls I wants for Christmas is a place to stay, a job that pays, and happiness all over my face. Am I dreaming?

"That sounds great to me. I will call you on Monday and make all of the arrangements." We shake hands. The smile on my face can be seen in LA, like the sun piercing through the smog. I am working. For some reason I start to move out of the door before the conversation between the principal and myself is done. Until I remember the paperwork in my hand, still blank. I stop moving my feet and try and keep my mind concentrated on his words and not the past. I know I want to go, now. Instead I take a seat and start filling out the paperwork, concentrating on my breathing and my thoughts.

"Hey Frederic, I just want you to know that I know that you will work hard for the students. And I also want you to know that I believe in what you did for those students at your last job. Without you there for them, who knows what might have happened to them." His eyes meet mine. I look away and resign from holding the weight of his gaze. I do not want to talk about my last job.

"Oh, I hope I did not bring up something that you might not want to discuss, I just wanted you to know as the leader of this institution I want someone like you here."

This time I meet his eyes and honor his words, attempting to hold back my own emotions. I feel my skin tighten, and the anxiety I was feeling disappears.

I muster up enough energy to speak.
"Thanks again. I am excited about being here, and I appreciate your words of encouragement. I truly do. I have been taking it slow in my healing in reference to my last job. I'm ready to get back in the classroom, and I think this is going to be a great place for me." All the strength I have in the world is holding me up, fighting back tears and enabling me the foundation to stand. I finish the paperwork and hand it back to him.

We shake hands, and I leave his office. His powder blue tie and green shirt are imprinted on my mind forever, the dimes in his loafers still shining.

I had not thought about my last job in a long time.

5:07 p.m. After the meeting with the principal, I walked slowly down the hallway. I wanted to feel each step as if it was my first. Knowing that each step was another step closer to my dreams. I couldn't hear any of students or any laughter as I walked down the cluttered hallway out of the school. I could only hear my heart beating faster than the Greyhound's tires this morning. Suddenly, I felt warm salty tears rolling down my brown kissed cheeks, into the corner of my mouth, down my throat.

Why am I crying?

Flashes of students running and screaming down a dark hallway. Soldiers, or police chase after students as the screams gain in frequency and pitch. Windows shatter as some students fall, others trampled on by angry stomping feet - soldiers. I'm standing there, helpless, it seems. I see someone running against the tsunami of students and officers forming in the long hallway. Smoke enters. Everything becomes blurry.

I rub my eyes and open them wide. I shake my head and try and forget the images. I'm standing in the middle of the sidewalk as people rush past me on either side. More tears pour out from my eyes. 'My soul was shedding her tears,' I thought. Letting out all that had been bottled up. I was working again.

And since, it's time to party.

"Someone got a straw?" I asked in a hurried cokehead fashion, looking at my fragmented reflection in the cocaine smeared mirror. 'What a long Friday' I thought to myself, as I looked at my cell phone and saw that it was two twelve in the morning, snorting two lines of coke into both nostrils, a line for each hour.

"What are you saying to me? We're here alone," Sonia laughs. Sonia had a long last name that I never remembered. I also used to lose her number a lot, too. I always thought the two things had something to do with each other. She was short, a little shorter than me; her breasts were full and when held in my hands gave me an instant hard-on. I think she was some kind of mixed breed, mother who was of Spanish gypsy origin, father who was North African. Born in Marseilles, France and raised with hundreds of different languages and people from all over the world, Sonia was one of the worldly types I never wanted to leave my side. She spoke of Marseilles as if it was heaven, a place where all of her points met. "Whoa!" I screamed, snorting up the lines of coke and passing the mirror and straw. Standing straight up and inhaling as if my life depended on it- feeling cool, miles davis cool, calm as my heart beat faster than the rotating wheels of the Greyhound, and this traveled life of mine. I start to do a jig to teddy pendergrass crooning to loving something or someone and take a gulp from my warm greyhound sitting on the cigarette littered table.

"Yeah, like I was saying there are so many beautiful people for you to meet on this planet. Go on, go. William is like some thick mud holding your feet down heavy. Freddie, you are so beautiful man, don't even trip. You are a treasure and William's just a slimy greedy pirate trying to keep you locked away from the rest of the world. Oh shit, you should come to Marseilles and meet one of those beautiful African boys out there, or even my brother. I know that would be weird fucking the whole family. You know you could have me, but not with me and my brother, that would be way too weird for me.. hahahaha" She said too fast, and forgot some of the words, as she finished off the rest of the powdery substance. We both looked into the misty mirror seeing a reflection of two people, four eyes, two noses and two sets of lips. We laugh out loud in unison.

"Freddie - kiss me. Right now, shit."

There's something motherly in the way she affectionately calls me "Freddie"; although, neither my mother, nor anyone else ever called me "Freddie."

We kiss for an eternity, and poetry writes itself on each of her nipples. As if my tongue was the pen. I guess it was my tongue, if I could only feel it. She jacks me off and grabs hold of my left nipple like he stole something from her, and for his crime she's gonna strangle the shit out of him. I like that though. So she continues to strangle. My fingers enter into her vagina and wetness seeps into me, soon after my tongue enters next; it is numb, wet and reaching for her deepest senses.

Her white face frightens me when I open my eyes, and she notices and smiles, pulling the right nipple now as I close my eyes again. Her head goes down to penis and she rubs her head against min_e. He grows silently giant, she holds him, me inside her warm mouth. I remember now that she has braces, and I think how she looked so much better before when she had crooked-messed up teeth. I casually switch positions with her and allow my numb tongue to re-enter her moist. Like serenades on hilltops from fleeting strangers, our feelings remain same. Juices escape from open mouths slowly crawling down chins into darkness. When she screams this time, I can feel and taste my tongue, sleep enters me.

When my alarm goes off on my relatively silent cell-phone, I am already late for class and a group of huge headaches have met and now live inside of my morning thoughts. Damn, I'm late, like a broken record, scratching back and forth again playing over the words, Damn, I'm late. Damn I'm late.

Damn

I'm

late.

I open my eyes and notices that she (Sonia) has left already, and I hurry on clothes and run out the door. The bus passes me, and I refuse to run. Remembering something my mother always said when a bus was close but too far to continue briskfully walking. "Shit, it'll be another one. Besides I don't be running after nothing, especially no bus and no nigga either.' I light a cigarette.

I don't think she wanted me to adopt this phrase as my own, especially the nigga part, but somehow it is quite fitting. When the bus arrives, I get on and sit in a corner seat. Now, I think how much I smell like sex, it must be pretty loud. I sit in the cuts of the empty bus and try and blend into the emptiness. I look outside the window and realize that I am in SF and not LA. I am not in school here. I'm just high. I also realize that I have quite a fu*king headache still! Damn, I'm not late.

I exit the bus at the next stop.

I sit on the stairs in front of the entrance to a random elementary school and open up my journal to write.

8/13/04

Damn, I must be f*cked up. I'm up early and ain't got no place to go for a minute. I think I left my keys for Jon's place in a sea of pillows on Sonia's floor. I'm all high and shit with nowhere to go. Maybe, I can find a way into her place somehow? Maybe?

I am afraid sometimes. Sometimes I am afraid. I also feel that fear is creeping up behind me sometimes. Memories are fearful. Fear is a disease with the self. An admittance that truth is not inherent, and faith no longer apparent, all hope seems to be wrapped up inside of my big empty head. When fear succumbs any of our senses, we dis-allow the flow to do just that, flow. By stepping out of the way and re-leasing the mis-conception that we control our own lives, we are able to make manifest that which is designed by god. I just wish I could accept something as truth. Our creations are that much more beautiful when designed in the stillness of that which is our creation. I always think that the way I live is in some ways balanced. Cyclical. I am strong at times. At times I am strong. When I am able to make sense of the webs I have weaved and their intricate meanings and accompanying belief systems, I become stronger still. This strength at times wavers because of the lack of continued confidence in myself. Maybe, because of all of the commitments that we don't honor with ourselves, we stop trusting our opinions and emotions and fall back on some kind of system that has worked in the past, but actually has no true relevance for the present moment. To sit back and view ourselves from the outside looking in: asking those hard questions of whether or not we would like ourselves if we met on the street.

I close my journal. Stick my pen in my pocket. I pick up the rest of my shit and leave, sniffling and snide at myself again, not because of my smell this time, but because I'm tired, sleepy, and have an aching head.

The weekend passes by like a blizzard in Chicago. Snow falling on every inch of me. Snow falling inside every inch of me, and without the shovel needed to clear a way, I am stuck in a snowstorm. Snow. Everywhere. Here comes the snow again, running up my nose like a melody…

----------------------mon. 7:30 a.m.----------------------

I'm starting to see more and more cocaine in my life. The last three nights have blended into wild explosions of sex, coke sex, like that sex you only get when you're coked up, all night long sex. And self-articulated coke talk, like any talk, it's just talk. *'blah, blah, fucking blah.* Erratic-emotional-release, lacking action and motivation and experience in these new terrains, I continue on my journey through the forests floor, each step a new admittance that I am possibly walking away from myself again. Of course, I found Sonia again, and we continued on our lovely rendezvous into each other's most intimate of spaces. But I never found Jon's keys.

8:15 a.m.

My cell phone rings.

8:28 am

I cried as I hung up the phone. The smiley-faced white guy with the compassionate eyes, stern handshake, and powder blue tie told me I did not have a job anymore because the district would not hire me. He mumbled something about my last job, and something about me not being welcomed back into any school inside of the district, ever. His voice was melancholic, like stinky ass gin - and I could hear the sadness creeping out of the receiver, like the smell from the Greyhound when I first arrived, oozing out onto the quiet unexpected morning streets of San Francisco. The record has been scratched. I am not working.

I am not working. I am not working. I am not....
working

It is still Monday.

For some reason, the phone conversation made me think that a whole day had passed, but it had not.

I take a line of coke. Since, Sonia had left for work, I decide to make another drink as well.

I take a shower and sit on the floor of Sonia's front room naked, my back still wet, alone with my drink and decide to take another line of coke. I decide to get dressed and walk to the Bart train station.

The first train to arrive at the station and I sleep walk into it. Find myself a window seat and look out into the window. I don't care which direction the train is going; I just need some kind of movement, anything to take me away from where my feet were.

Like a rock thrown into a glass menagerie, shattering the stillness, the inherent beauty therein. I need warmth. I am breaking. Each piece of me, breaking, shattering into tiny pieces, breaking, apart of. Not the glass, but the breaking of the rock. The splintering of civilizations, strength and fortitude slowly crumbling from the top down, crumbling from the inside out, atop of my head. They say addiction runs in the family, and I do not even have to listen to what they say in order to know this is true. I'm in the race. Or, I'm in the running. The addiction, I guess, is what is hereditary. The running is constant. The state of our society leads to drugs. I'm forced to say this because there is definitely a disconnect that is antagonized and promoted by the systems that be. Like the system is fucked up and so, we take drugs to cope with that fucked up system, and then the system in turn wants to further fuck us up by criminalizing the very remedy that actually works.

Looking desperately for something to catch my attention, I stare out, eagerly, from the train window. Trees flash past and colors escape sight just as fast as trees. I try to hold on to something, the bitter taste of her moist womb still lingering from last night. Anything. Some sort of warm feeling from the smiley-faced white man. A leg or foot tangled under the weight of a passenger sitting in front of me on the speeding greyhound. Something. I start to think about my Friday to Monday exploits and there is one thing that permeates each day, my attention, at least now. I pull out my journal and try to write. cocaine.

white lines, an 80's song
the radio's volume max was 10
mine pushed heaven. if truth exists,
her name is music. thin legged, but big boned. her waist

cocked to the side ready to rhythm.

it was the mid to late 80's
and music and capitalism and drugs fucked all day long in a
orgy for the times, ny/ all world- long

empire state
of mind.

into the long muted, and abated night, wetness escaped into
the atmosphere
habits and huxtibles piled up high as
cocaine mountains magesty – reagan**thatcher**nomics-
red light green light yellow light -
GO!

no wonder this retro 80's thing coincides with a resurgence
of coke, soft money, inflation, deficits and 80's music

(to be sung) whitelines going through my head
(to be sung) whitelines going through my head
(to be sung) whitelines running up my nose
(to be sung) whitelines running up my nose

and debts building/cause they say the party is over.

the party's not over

the party's not over

and debts building/cause they say the party has ended.

the radio's volume max was 11

mine pushed heaven. if truth exists

her name is music. thin legged, big boned. high waist

cocked to the side ready to rhythm

2.

wearing all white, she moves past me like a cold wind off

of lake Michigan waters.

her waist always enticing, always inviting

always a long time before i come

                                          back home
                                          to myself
                        I fall, inside her syrupy sweets
          Engulfed in a-mud hut, calling ancestors home

What am I going to do? At the end of the line, Daly City

train, and no apparent destination, I can't even think of

anything but escape. I cross over the platform and wait for

the train going the opposite direction. As I stand facing the direction of the coming train I think about my party crashing entrance back home to San Francisco.

I smile briefly and laugh when I think about losing a job I barely even had. The sardonic way it happened so fast and the chilling similarity to losing William. I get to LA, and I lose William. I get to San Francisco; I lose job.

I look into the encroaching, approaching distance, like horizons. I think of Zora Neale Hurston's opening lines in her famous novel, *Their Eyes Were Watching God.*

Ships at a distance have every man's wish on board. For others they sail forever on the horizon, never out of sight, never landing until the Watcher turns his eyes in resignation, his dreams mocked to death by Time. That is the life of men.

*J.B. Lippincott & Co. 1937

Promised promises. When the train arrives I step in. Not quite the ship Zora spoke of, but it will have to suffice. I sit by a window and search with my eyes for anything to keep my attention, a tree or a building, or a passing Greyhound bus in route.

drink #2

When I wake up, I am nearly crushed by a huge blind man being led by what looks to be another blind person. Immediately, 'the blind leading the blind', enters my head, I laugh uncontrollably as I dart out of the way before his fat ass lands on my lap. Ughh. I smile and chuckle a bit more wondering what time it is.

My eyes stare out into the evening's mystery, as dusk enchants night's entrance. I wait to see what the next stop will be and notice that I must have slept two whole train routes, back and forth, from Daly City to Concord, and back again. My mind tells me that I am fucked. I rummage through the emptiness of my brain (most of what had remained probably stolen by a bum as I slept) and wonder if I have anyone that I can call. Not like I am desperate, but I am still pretty fucked up, and it would be nice to know where I am going to sleep tonight. Names on my cell phone scroll up and down until I realize that I have a friend who I definitely need to call. A feeling of relief enraptures me and I look through my bag searching for two Tylenols that I find, underneath conjunctions, in the corner of my mess of a bag. I pull the lint off of them and throw them both in my mouth. I use whatever saliva remains in my mouth to swallow the pills.

The train pulls into Orinda station.

Wiping away the matching crust in my eyes and mouth, I exit the train and straighten my clothes. "Is anybody looking at me?" I ask out loud confirming that I still have my voice. I wonder what I must look like. "Why?" I reply to myself. I feel like I don't know where I am. It's been four days since I left LA, and of course I still care what I look like. Living in LA made me more self-conscious than I've ever been. Every time I left the house I sat in the mirror for what seemed to be hours, making sure every thing was absolutely fabulous. You never know when the paparazzi are near by looking for a beautiful black man like me to immortalize through print.

The phone rings for what seems to be dreadfully too close to an eternity. I feel my blood rising. Not because I am nervous but I know he will answer. I know he will come and get me. All this I know, and it makes me feel safe for some reason. Like, at least tonight, will be alright.

Bryan answers.

'Bienvenidos, amigo. Hey, what ya doing?' Bryan grunts.
He sounds like he is watching some sport channel in his
sweats, five beers down, not even looking at what's on the
screen. I tell him to come and get me from the train station.
I wait, filling the empty time with my thoughts like a
forgotten child waiting for a parent at the curb after school.

"I thought you had somewhere to go, or something about
staying with Jon and going to his birthday party?" he says,
barely audible.

I repeat, "Come get me from the train, man. I want to see
you, plus, I got laid off today, so company with a good
friend would be kind of cool, huh? You want to see me,
don't you?" Hoping I don't sound too desperate, I wait for
Bryan's answer with my feet crossed, one over the other,
for good luck.

He laughs, says yes, and hangs up the phone.

For some reason I don't even think about Jon past the mention of his name. I should call him, I think to myself, but am bombarded by thoughts of Bryan.

Bryan's dark skin always enraptures me, conjures me into a spider's webbing. Something about being mixed with anything Black always intrigues me. I think it's like the saying, the darker the berry the sweeter the juice. Black juice makes everyone sweeter. And Bryan was fine as hell. He made me want to take him into a dark corner and fuck the shit out of him, I mean, we never did - but damn, I thought about his Black and Filipino ass all the time. All the things I could do to him and what I imagined he would do to me. I guess sometimes I am a bit of a whore, not like the ones in the movies, or on the street corners, but one like me. I like to fuck, to be held under a spell of some kind of lustful encounter, something to make me forget. Only to remember that the act alone takes me to a new space inside of me, a cool calming space inside of me.

The moment is our creation. Our web we weave. Wanting nothing more than to crawl up his web and live there. Spiders we are. Able to levitate and land where our web finds us; most times out in thin air. His lips look as if they

were african and filipino brothers dancing the night away
under a full moon, entangled in a kiss. His lips, thick,
brown molasses lingering on mine; buckwheat pancakes,
large and brown, flapping in the syrupy sweet of his cool.

miles davis. cool.

I don't know why I always equate cool with miles davis; I guess it's a jazz thing. Black virtuosos in suits, holding their weapons of musical equality and funking up the arrangements with improvisation only Africans can do. We've totally lost our concept of cool since jazz has declined in popularity over the years. If you don't believe me ask a young person to define cool, it's kind of sad. Bryan and I never kissed. Never did anything for that matter. I told you I used to think of him all the time, and I did. Imagined how our bodies would fit together, how he would hold me, and how I would be held by him. I never remember where Bryan and I met. But, I do remember always loving him. He was one those people who loved James Baldwin, and Miles Davis, equally as much I did. We would have great conversations about jazz and literature, in general, but I think when it came specifically to the love we both had for Baldwin and Davis - we would find intersections and similarities that even surprised us. We shared some kind of conversational spaghetti junction. I think we always loved each other, but we were both in relationships at the time. I didn't always use to be such a whore. Now that we both are officially single, I'm excited to see what happens. I'm fucking thrilled he answered the phone.

I stare into the clouds as a tear falls from my eyes. Like a snowflake, no tear is the same. Laughing as I wipe the tears from my cheek, I search again in my bag, meandering for a cigarette this time. I find a broken cigarette, put it together again, and light it. I pull the fumes in, blow them out - breathe them in and blow them out, a smoky residue of cool. *Fiberglass and ammonia, tar and nicotine; not the saxophone blast I so long for, but I guess it'll do.*

Searching through my head for something else to think about, but always landing right back at the lost job and my life that seems to be practically falling through my grasp. I fucking came all the way here on a busted ass Greyhound bus "not" to get a job? You ever have those times when life happens to you in a way where you would have never in a million years believed the events that actually happened were even possible? Fuck.

Drag after drag of my fractured cigarette reveals new problems, other things to think about. Like the fact that my bank account has been negative for more than a month, and I have no money.

They gonna close that account. Like they did the last one and I will be assed out again. Why they be messing with a black man like that? I guess I'm gonna have to call my mama.

Before I lose all of my senses, Bryan pulls up in a Black drop top something or other. I've never been into cars, as far as brand names and all that, I just like driving in them. Actually, I just like getting rides in them. I jump in the car like Starsky and Hutch used to do, feet first through the window. I'm Starsky, and he's Hutch.

'What the fuck?' Bryan says, jumping back and swinging at my legs with his massive forearm. I just laugh as we speed away.

'It's a fucking convertible, d_ick. Stop your shouting. You're supposed to jump in like that! Haven't you ever watched Starksy and Hutch?' I poke Bryan in the side, and we both laugh.

Bryan motions to his ashtray and I look down to see a joint rolled to perfection, ready to get smoked. I light it up and feel Bryan's paternal hand on my knee. I think to myself how cool this is. Bryan is exactly where I want to be, fast and furious. Don't you hate it when you are with someone, both got mad energy for each other, but no one makes the first move - so the whole entire night is spent kind of bull-shitting through small talk and other shit? I totally hate that. I lean back as his hand, no longer paternal, now loving, begins to move slowly towards my penis. I like marijuana. I like hands. I like hands on my peni_s.

you got a fast car, is it fast enough so that we can drive away...
forever?

*Elektra Records 1988

Maybe, this is life. Small portions of good feelings wrapped up in the darkness of what life truly is, a fucking disappointment. But I'm an aesthetician, and it fills me up to see beautiful things, packages. I think the word is "Asawe", a connoisseur of beautiful things. I kind of don't even care what's inside the packages sometimes. The excitement of the colorful gift-wrapping paper and the wonder of what is possibly inside of the package always holds my attention.

My peni_s begins to grow, and I pass the joint to Bryan. His hand feels so good that I wish it would never move. A hand on my dick everywhere I walked. What would that look like walking into the bank to withdraw money? Would people even say anything to me? Bryan's like almost six feet tall, and I'm about five feet seven inches, so the sight would be something to see.

I stare into his brown face. Bryan is black Filipino beauty.

the wind blows through me and i enter a dream. clouds and stars appear before me. i am standing naked surrounded by other naked men and women staring into the moon. we all lower our heads in syncopation and i look around and notice that all the faces are faces of people i have had sex with or wanted to in the past. they are smiling and so am i.

for some reason, i am not angry with anyone. i begin to dance. everyone else starts to move their waists and hips, arms and legs. we all begin to find the rhythm in far away spaces that we have ignored when we were just having sex. instead of lusting over our bodies and then covering up our bodies, we are able to share in the lovely features and intricacies of ourselves in our birth form. completely naked with no guilt and no shame associated with our various forms and inconsistent sizes, we all begin to move and groove, as god begins to clap and stomp her feet, the master orchestra leader, directing the movements of our instruments, our bodies. we follow the stomping as tears begin to fall from all of our eyes, it is raining inside, a pool. the tears have formed a pool. instead of using the image of the naked body for sexual fantasies or selling cars, we are able to see the reflection of ourselves in each other. as more and more tears fall, we begin to see our images in the huge pool below. narcissus, speaks to the lake, we get lost in our own images of ourselves, our bodies moving, the lake speaks back. vanity and god's feet orchestrating a rhythm, and her children smiling at the sight of giving alms for everything we have experienced, good and bad.

I wake from my nap and realize that we are at Bryan's

house already. The joint has been smoked, and my hard penis is still, hard. Bryan's hand moves to put the car in park.

He always makes me feel like I am important.
It's like Bryan was the guy that I could talk to about William. It seemed like Bryan always understood me. He dated men and women, like me, and I think we both had a secret crush on each other when we first became friends. We never called ourselves bi-sexual or gay, something about labeling ourselves felt base and unauthentic, you know? The fact that we did not just start having sex with each other helped us remain friends this long.

When I first met him I didn't like him at all. It wasn't exactly love at first sight, or even like at first sight. I just thought he was too nice to be for real. With all the craziness I used to get from gay men in the past, either trying to just fuck or too uppity and pretty to even be looked at, Bryan was an oxymoron. Fine ass hell, and a nice guy too. Guess I just thought he was fake or something, not real. How could a gay guy, who looked like him, be this nice? Needless to say, after I got over myself, Bryan and I became great friends.

When we enter the house, Bryan leads me. He holds me, and I feel like my father has returned. The whole issue with fatherless children and those of us who were queer finding father in male lovers was somewhat of a trip to me. His clothes seem to shed by osmosis: mine do the same. When he grabs me, I feel his penis near my thigh, and I smile. I close my eyes and allow his strong arms to envelope me. Man holding man; Bryan holding Frederic. I want to give myself up to the insatiable feeling to unite to something tangible, something real. Something hard- like this dic_k in my hand, against my tongue, in my mouth.

i feel warm and the winds outside asks me to be still. the trees' limbs push silently against the windowpane as the heat from his body makes me warmer. pushing still his penis enters me, like the limbs against the windowpane, wood against glass, fragile. softly- back and forth, like a deserted melody, passionately obscure, relatively obtuse, honestly speaking. our hearts beat together in syncopated handclaps; the choir is sweating. it's hot in church this sunday morning. the preacher has pulled out her handkerchief more than three times. halleluia, amen. can the choir say amen! the penal gland, i mean the choir, is feeling the spirit.

Bryan reaches to his bureau and opens a drawer. He grabs two yellow pills with smiley faces on them and closes his hand.

"Open your mouth."
"You gonna put your dick back in it?" Laughing uncontrollably, I slowly open my mouth. Bryan drops an ecstasy pill in my mouth and then drops one in his. He grabs a bottle of water sitting by the bed and hands it to me. I gulp a huge mouth full and pass it back to Bryan.

"Okay then." I slap Bryan on the thigh and lean my head on his torso.
"Your black ass is fine Frederic, man. You know how good you look in the dark." He says. I smile and lay my head in his lap; I look up into his eyes and begin to cry. He traces my naked body with his right hand.

"What's up with these tears? Don't start crying when I give you some ecstasy boy. 'Man up boy!' he mocks. His face looks at me less teasingly. "You know I'm just joking, but

I tell you looking all good in the dark, and you gonna cry on me? What you gon' do when I tell you, you ugly?"

"Nothing. It's not that. I mean, I'm happy and all. It's just I'm rarely happy Bryan. There are intense moments like these where I feel happy, but rarely do I feel happiness, I mean feel anything for that matter. It's just I feel a bit disoriented. I just got here a few days ago, been through the wire and back, and now I'm here with you. And I love being here with you. It's just what I wanted when I called. It's what I wanted since the first time we met, not actually the first time, but you know what I mean. The thoughts I've had for so long coming true exactly when I need something in my life to actually happen right. I just feel like this is the first time we have been together, and now we're both single. It's like we were virgins to each other just now.

I gave you something, parts of myself that I do not want back. We are both aware of parts of me, and spaces inside of you, that we can use to make something together. We are both single right now, you get it? Right now, we just made love. For the first time having sex tonight! You get it? (without pause) It felt like we had been together before, not the actual truth of this being our first time even touching. It was so easy. And, I just feel so far away right now. Like I am not even here. Like there is still something that is holding me back. Like the blackness you see is not me, but a hole in which everything else rests. I guess that is why I feel so far away." Sometimes I hear myself and think I'm way too dramatic for my own self. Scarlett O'Hara ain't got shit on me.

"Frederic, I think you think too much. I think ever since that thing happened with the school district you have been a little different, you know? And for good reason. You also lost your man right after you left to LA to be with him. I mean the mutha-fucka asked you to move with him to take some of the pressure off from the school shit, and then he only adds more pressure by fucking leaving you? I didn't want you to go in the first place, but I saw how happy you were when he asked you to come. I also saw how sad you were after you were arrested. It seemed like the only thing to make you happy back then was William. So, it's understandable—I understand—if you're a bit confused sometimes. You've been through a lot baby. Also, I think you probably feel so far away because we just had amazing sex, and now we bout to be high as all hell on ecstasy. You know? Some good MDMA. So, I get it bruh, I really do."

He wipes the tears from my face, and we both laugh. We are about to be pretty high, I say.

We both laugh uncontrollably. Bryan smiles and grabs hold of me real hard. I surrender in his arms. I know that it will all be all right - soon enough – but definitely tonight. Shit, right now. Electricity is coming out of his hands into my body. The sweat on our bodies cooled from the fan in the window and every nerve in my naked body begins to stand up on end.

Something in his naked-ness makes me feel clothed. I feel warm, finally. There is a sense of protection in his arms. He hums Miles Davis' *blue and green* and I explode. We look into each other's eyes, and I see Bryan's innocence. You know that space in someone when you don't need to know anything, cause all you know is everything? That quiet companion who has been along the journey the whole time as just an observer, now as I lay my head against his hairy chest, I know I am here for a reason. I know he is more than an observer, he is a co-pilot, a friend, a sexy beast; and I want him to take me away.

what if a dream was not deferred but granted and
something could go right in my life for a change. as of late,
i feel like everything has fallen through my hands, like sand
from a broken hour glass game piece. part of me does not
even want to think about why i lost the job. another part of
me wants to fight for the job and go head-to-head against
that dumb ass district Superintendent, while another part
wants to get the fuck out of san francisco, again, quick. but
where? i just got here. it's like it's all coming back up
again. the issues from the past, the fact that the institution I
used to work for kicked me out for protecting my students.
Now, they don't want me back, again?

again. bryan was right - i have changed since the school
thing. i am stagnant right now, like feet in concrete, all the
way to my knees at times. i just sit inside new situations and
allow them to take over the melancholic time and the base,
banal parts of life. what was I thinking trying to work in a
school again? people become such a great distraction
from dealing with those issues in life we cannot seem to
handle. what happens if an issue knocks you out and it's
hard to get up and you don't feel like getting out of bed
again? what happens if I crash? what happens then? or
when you cannot enter a classroom again because you are

*too afraid? those muthafuckas ain't got the nerve to tell me
in my face. they gots to get a wimp ass white man in a
powder blue shirt to shatter my dreams on a monday
morning, and on the phone, even. who even wears impotent
ass powder blue anymore?*

*i wonder what other people are thinking when they are with
me. i can be lying with someone, doing drugs and talking a
mile per second and at the same time be inside a whole
other world in my thoughts. i learned this from growing up
with my mother. my mother. i have to call her. i need some
money.*

I feel the e kicking in. MDMA is a lovely drug. A
happiness injection, a fluid wave toward mother's ocean.
The sensation finds spaces in every angle of Bryan's body.
Each muscle is searing hot, temperatures rising inside of
me as well. I breathe into my lungs and feel light as air.
Actually, I feel as if I can fly.
So, I do.
Fly into Bryan's body, arms shaped like the nose of a
plane, I aim directly for his chest. It feels like a crash
landing as Bryan falls backward into the mountain of
pillows behind him in slow motion. I lie inside Bryan, but

I'm just atop of his naked body. Bryan and I feel like one
sound,
one beat,
a melody playing above, sung by the angels who have
planned this night.

Right now I'm in love with Bryan's hand_s and his
understanding of the male body and its forms and its
intrigue. I'm soup as he stirs. I'm dough as he makes me
into bread. He is a master potter, and there is something to
be said about the skill and ability of someone creating
works of art with their hands out of the clay of my body.
Somehow the feeling of being molded, stretched and folded
is all I need to morph into his creation. And I think the e is
helping with me as metaphor. I linger long and hard on the
beauty of his body, lying elongate across the sands of my
imagination. Caught in mid-thought I forget everything and
enter him presently.

*i wants to eat him, internalize this feeling forever, eat him
and have him with me in all places, eat him and have him
with me in all situations. eating him, knowing that all is
well with his arms around me, inside out of me. i think that
maybe i could relax with him, if i eat him, maybe not. i*

would not want to digest him, but eternally taste him. savor him. roll his sweet flavor inside my mouth, and let all the juices sit there in my mouth. but i could just lay there, here in his arms, making new names for us, creating new avenues of thought. as high as i am right now, i feel grounded. like my feet are on the ground for the first time.

I roll around inside him and escape again in the winter months of a situation. Hibernating in the snow-covered peaks on the horizon of his body's terrain like deserted islands and salt mines, pyramids and mouths of rivers. Men's bodies are so different than women's. There are so many intricacies of the body and every body varies immensely, and tragically speaking - can only belong to the owner, if you get my drift.

I fucked a woman who was a man once, and I was so mad because all the while they told me they was a woman, and stories about growing up a little girl, and I believed them. After all the lies, they turned out to have a dick. He was hiding his dick and it fell out from hiding when he got all caught up in the feeling of sex. I was mad cause I thought I was fucking a woman and then a dick falls from nowhere. Don't get me wrong I like dicks, of course. But I like them when I like them. When I want some vaginal time that's what I want - anyway, a tangent is ending.

Come to think of it, lately, the only woman I have slept with is Sonia. Since I was raised in a heterosexual world, I thought I was supposed to be with only women. Dating them made me feel so inadequate. There always seemed to be so many rules, hold the door, walk on the outside of them when out in the world, so in case a car is driving out of control and drives on the sidewalk, I get crushed. Or pay for everything and drive everywhere. No thank you. I hated driving, and didn't have a car anyway. And more important, I didn't have no money anyway. I always wondered who was gonna pay for Frederic? Needless to say, I realized quite early on that I was ill equipped to be this man of adventure, the one who could protect them against every ill and runaway car in the world.

It's as if the remainder of the night into morning, our childhoods meshed together for safety. I helped Bryan as he loses step, falls over some sad moments of his early years. He strokes my cheek as I remember moments alone without knowing when company or protection would come. We hold unto each other and sympathize with one another about the love we both had hoped would come but never did.

We feel good together. Whether it's the drugs or the requiem of our love, we belonged together tonight. We made love to our pain and healed it in some strange way. At least we hoped we had. We wake up the next day around noon. It feels good to sleep in a little, to have such a large man holding me, especially when I have felt quite broken lately.

By two o'clock, Bryan is gone. When I awake, I rub the sleep from my eyes and maneuver myself into the bathroom to brush my teeth and take a shower.
I see my naked body in the long mirror on the way to the bathroom. I stop and stare at myself.
I trace my naked body with my hands.
I look at each of my fingers in the mirror against my brown skin.
Fingers, branches share a familiar life.
arms
chest, waist, hips
legs, thighs,
dic_k, always stiff, it seems. Ready for something.

I point my toe and watch my calf muscle flex up and down, and back up again. Vision myself ballerina. I enter the shower, pirouette and all.

The water lands on my head like a waterfall above, sharing its sparkling gifts of wetness on the dryness of my yesterday, and I can hear resounding truths crashing, dancing against the backdrop of this painting. The colors are changing. I had been feeling autumn in my veins, but now springtime enters, and I feel like a new day, a new year. It's amazing how a good fuck can make me feel like spring, anew. A new leaf, fallen from the tree. A new penis or finger entering my rectum, touching my penal gland, a rhythm I'm hearing –an understanding, a searing Nina Simone song sung throughout every part of me. Exit the shower, dry my ass off - run to the front room to turn the television on.

Bryan has cable and 'ON DEMAND'. That channel is so amazing to me. Real amazing technology. It's all the shows whenever you want them. I watch *six feet under* all day long. I fall asleep naked on the couch, a melted bowl of ice cream on the floor. Pink shaving cream. When I wake up, it is later, much later. Still naked, I stand in front of the toilet and piss yellow hot fever. I need to drink some water, soon. I cup my hands and drink as many small hands full of water that I can drink without feeling sick. I fill my hollowed stomach with heavy sink water.

I fall asleep watching videos. There are videos on so many channels. I try to catch up on all the videos I never saw in LA, but heard about because everyone I knew was in them. I flip from bet to mtv, vh1 to mtv2, mtv espanol to vh1soul, and finally mtv urban.

Finally I get dressed.

Sitting on the couch, staring at myself in the mirror across from me, there seems to be a change that has happened. I sit there for five minutes, and then I grab my coat from the closet.

Before I leave I write Bryan a note.

I open the door and stand lost in early evening sunset. Lost in the image, I am standing in the middle of my life. Knowing not which way I am going, still I begin walking somewhere. But I know that I am moving forward. No matter what I thought I had lost, there is always something new to be gained around the corner. Almost as if the thing that we lose is lost because the thing that we must acquire is on the way or here already, and if we don't pay attention to the loss, we may never find what we were looking for. Both phenomena cannot exist in the same space at the same time. So, if we had received that thing that we thought we lost, we really would have lost something else we obviously needed right? Huh?

It's confusing, but I think I got it. Like I was supposed to lose that job to gain something. I get caught up in the something to be gained and want to gain it, right now! Which in a way is denying the humility that accompanies this type of gift if we have the patience. These gifts come when we are able to be still and accept the possibility of the moment. Patience.

Anyway, I know that there is something coming that is much more desirable than that job I lost.

On the train, I pull out, 'The Prophet", by Kahlil Gibran, and begin to look for the chapters on love and beauty. Both make me smile and take me internal. I start to think about quitting smoking, and cocaine, shit drugs in general.

Basically quitting all my frivolous habits of expense. I decide against making such a rush decision. I can't make a decision like this, right now. Can I? I need to look at this strategically. I answer no; it's an obvious answer. He smiles. I laugh. (Who he is? My addiction I guess.)

I start to write in my journal about my crash course return to the bay area. It has definitely been quite a bumpy ride back. I mean who would have thought just five days ago, I was on a cramped Greyhound bus with my eyes on a new job, an apartment and a Will-free existence. Now, I am on the train again, no place to live, but with more optimism than I had before I came here. Even if it is synthetic, right?

'I better go get my bags from Jon's house and bring them back to Bryan's?' I think out loud. I have not talked to Jon since the first minutes I'd been in town. If I had any sense about myself I would remember what it is that I forgot regarding Jon's house and plans we had made. But, right now I am all that I can think about. I have to make sure I'm okay, and then I can figure the rest of this stuff out later.

(time code?):
Dear Journal

So situations have landed me in another space. Again, I feel
lost.

I pull out my black marker and draw 2 lines through the
bullshit I had started to write in my journal.
~~*Dear Journal*~~
~~*So situations have landed me in another space. Again, I feel*~~
~~*lost.*~~
I want to be more honest, but nothing comes to my head. I
just hover over the page, pen in hand, equipped and ready
for battle. But no war with the page, no words at all, not
even a small respectable fight. I close my book and place
the pen in my pocket.
I exit the train.

If I am totally honest, something that has not happened for
quite some time, I've never ever healed from the school
incident. A part of me doesn't want to heal, or even know
how. I barely even have words for it. It was kind of like a
dream. The fact that I spent the majority of my life inside
of the school system, outside of the long arm of the law,
only to get arrested inside of a school, my only known
home. Something extremely sardonic about all of this
doesn't make me laugh, but definitely makes me think. I

know the black man is public enemy number one on the streets, but now with police officers stationed inside of schools, there are no more safe heavens, no where to run. *(Forget about safety; forget about it.)*

The day started like every school day for me. I didn't really want to go into school on this particular Friday. I was teaching a class on Malcom X, and oddly enough we were watching the film X, by Spike Lee. A student happened to look out of the window and started to scream something inaudible. I didn't know what she said, but the entire class stood up and ran to the window, myself included. There were police cars everywhere, like a river streaming from the entrance to the school all the way down to the street leading to the busy intersection which led to campus. Immediately, I told my teacher's aid to watch the students, and I ran downstairs to see what was going on. I thought someone must have been shot, or worst, dead.

When I got to the first floor, there was a sea of young people running, screaming, looking terrified. I still get chills when I think about it. As I moved through the sea of students, I noticed police officers chasing students through the hall way, two officers had pulled their guns out and had a line of students in handcuffs along the hallway wall. I tried to ask the police officers what was going on, but no one would tell me anything. Even the teachers were shocked, frozen in their tracks, watching the mele, as everything seemed to be moving in slow motion. I ran to the Principal's office and watched as the Police Chief held a female student by her pants belt buckle. Luckily I got to the door as he tossed her out of the doorway into my awaiting arms.

Catching the young girl, who was in hysterics, and confronting the Chief made matters worst. He began using profanity at me, and we exchanged a few heated words as I pushed him aside and ran into the office. Inside the Principal's office the chilling reality that the police were brutalizing my students became more obvious to me.

Three officers had one male student on his knees, and in handcuffs. Each officer exchanged blows on the young man's back, legs and neck. Adults looked on and said nothing, frozen like the other teachers in the hallway. I heard my voice scream STOP! The officers continued, the faces of the administration stayed frozen, and my heart stopped beating. I continued to scream, and no one said a word. It seemed like nothing would make the officers stop beating the young man, and I felt like I had to make a decision. I ran from the office and up three flights of stairs to the media lab. I grabbed a digital video camera and ran back down to the first floor.

Watching the events through the camera created more of a surreal feeling inside of me. I filmed the students in the handcuffs on the floor, the police officers chasing students through the hallway, teacher's hiding behind their classroom doors, and the incident that got me arrested.

When the police noticed that I had a camera, they began to set me in their sights as the one to stop. I hadn't noticed what happened until I was surrounded by police officers. Three officers yelled at me to drop the camera. When I pulled my face away from the camera, a fist punched me in the back of my head and another one hit me in the mouth simultaneously. I don't know how I kept hold of the camera, but somehow I did. It was a miracle that the camera did not break, or fall from my hand for that matter. I crashed hard against a locker and fell to my knees.

Somehow I got up as soon as my knees hit the ground and leaped to my feet, running up the nearest hallway staircase. Hearing the feet of six to ten officers now I ran for dear life. As I got to the second floor, the Principal was there with the Police Chief and two other officers. They must have run upstairs through another stairwell. I was trapped. All I remember next is hearing the Principal blame me for the altercation between the officers. She repeated that I was to blame for the ruckus happening, and she was extremely upset with me. I remember saying something to her about her inadequacy as the head of this institution. In my mind I still had no idea why the police were there in the first place. The police chief ordered the cops to detain me and grab the camera. I screamed for them to give me back the camera as they pulled my hands behind my back, and cuffed me. My head began to scream louder than I did, louder than my children in the hallways, and I blacked out, falling down a flight of stairs.

Standing on the train platform, my cell phone rings and it is Bryan.

"Hey. I hope you had a good day today. I was thinking, maybe it would be good if you stayed with me for a while. I like your company, a lot, and I have a lot of room in my place for the both of us. I think it would be good for us. We can get to know each other better!" Bryan's phone call is cryptic and necessary right now. I don't even think of anything else, but yes.

"That sounds good…" I say. "I was on the way to where my bags are hanging out. I'll go and get my stuff and be back over there tonight." Even though that's what I was hoping to do anyway.

"Cool. You want me to come and get you? Where you at?"

"That's okay. I'll get my stuff from Jon and come through. You're doing so much as it is. Thanks. I think I can at least manage to get to your house. Maybe, we can just hang out tonight. Relax for a bit, rent a movie and you know, hang out."

"That sounds really great. I guess I'll see ya at the house. Peace baby."

"Peace Bryan."

I hang up the phone and walk down 5th st. My cell phone rings again, and it is my mother. I push silence and throw the phone back into my bag.

I need to speak with her but not now. I want to just walk down the street and sing. Feel the blessing that came from the shell of this nutty ass weekend. An explosive entry back home, head first into the whirlwind of the San Francisco bay. The crisp winds are not crisp for nothing. The SF winds remind me of the tumultuous undertaking living can be when we are growing up in the big city. All the people and all the lights; a chilling reflection of what we have become, when the lights are the only brightness we are accustomed to seeing. At times, they can be blinding.

The cold downtown air catches a tear and flings it, left to fend for itself in the busy San Francisco streets. Cars and busses, horns and whores, chess players, businessmen, homeless people, thugs, b-boys and b-girls litter the animated pavement. Laughter screams from my chest. I am loud outside of my head. I don't have a job, but I do have me, and a place to lay my head. I smile.

I walk with my hands in my pocket, searching for some warmth. I get on the bus. The 14 Mission will take me to Jon's house to get my bags. I have not even spoken to him since I arrived at his pad and left all of my stuff on his floor. I hope Jon's not mad.

I dial Jon's number.

"he-l-lo." Jon echoes.
"Hey, what's up?"
"Man, I thought you were dead." Jon's voice sounds really anal and judgmental, like my mother, without the expectant need to be respectful, my response is harsh and quick to defend.
Just like Jon, serious, stoic and judgmental. I usually don't take too much of his shit, but I know I messed up this time.

"What do you mean?"
"Um, what the fuck do you think I mean man?" Jon never swears.
"You come in my house for about fifteen minutes and leave your stuff here in the middle of my front room since Friday morning; it's Tuesday evening Frederic. I mean I think it would have been nice to talk to you. I don't know where

you've been. Should I have waited for you these past five days? I thought you might want to talk to me and catch up. Maybe, since you said you would help me around the house. And I think we made plans for Saturday night. Did you forget my fucking engagement party?"

"Hey man, I'm so sorry. I Just got caught up."
OMG! Engagement party for Jon. That's what Bryan meant about a birthday party. Shit. I'm feeling really bad now. Like, I didn't even think about Jon at all. I just dropped my shit off and was ghost.

"Well…I want you to take your bags and your stuff and all of your shit out of my house, immediately. Yea, get the fuck out. I hope you have a place to go or something, because I am not going to put up with this anymore. You coming back is suppose to be this big whoa for everybody and you treat me like this, where have you been?" Jon's voice sounded really upset, and the whole scenario made me feel really sour.

"I….. was… with…."

"Well, I'll drop you where ever you want to go, but then that's that. I think I want to act like you're not here, like when you first left. It was hard, but this is not something to miss. Having a friend who would rather hang out with his loser friends than someone who loves and cares for him like a friend should. But, do the drugs, have the fun. I'll wait here for you to come and get your stuff. How long will it take you?"

"C'mon man, I have so much to tell you. Don't you think you're taking this a little far Jon? I'm so sorry, why all this negativity." I wished I had never called him. Just popped up to Jon's house when he was at work or something and grabbed my shit, leave a note, be a ghost for real.

"Frederic, seriously, I want you to come and get your bags." This time Jon's voice was loud and cracking. I think he's crying.

"Jon, are you crying? (pause, long and uncomfortable). Okay, here I come. If it's any consolation, I'm.."

The phone hung up hard, only silence filled my thoughts and the phone line. I thought about my friendship with Jon and the huge hole that was forming in my stomach. Jon was my friend from childhood, someone who was always there for me.

I found Jon again by accident. We were both entering my favorite café in the Mission district. Café Boheme, named after the opera with a similar feel. Smooth, dark, rich, dense colors, filling the air with hip movement, quite the place to meet artists from all walks of life. A morning at café Boheme was like living through the history of the bay area. Old revolutionaries, new griots and artists, community folks and coffee met my nose each day with excited fervor for the possibilities and the impenetrable cultural and social link between the past and the present. The lyrical notion of the bay area, with its radical posture and jazzy improvisation, a language that once you know it, find it really hard to ever forget.

When I saw Jon, I wiped my eyes and thought I must be still sleep. We hadn't seen each other in like six years. We both grew up on the north side of Chicago, both with single moms, no pops and no body but each other. Jon was like my own reflection, myself. He represented everything my mother wanted me to be. And at one point I had been all of those things; they just became too much for me to carry.

Everyone else's image(s) of me looked muddled, fragmented, and a distortion when compiled and assembled. I had no idea what I was supposed to do with all of these expectations. So, I did nothing with them, let me come into one ear and out the other.

Unlike these ideals, Jon and I had a friendship that was not about comparisons and contrasts. We were just friends. Synergy, interaction, collaboration; true hermanos. When we met again at Café Boheme, we never strayed again. We stayed in contact for years after, and he became one of my dearest friends, again. I think it was when his mother passed that we really became close. Since she was his only present parent, it was hard for him to lose her. After she passed I think the only thing that comforted him was the heaps of money she left him in her will. Whenever he felt sad and missed her, he would buy something. From property to whole collections of music from Prince, or the Beatles, even though he already owned it on his laptop, he would buy the physical cds and eventually give them away as gifts to friends.

I would never want to hurt Jon. Damn, from Sonia to Bryan, I just got lost somewhere. Maybe, he will talk to me when I get there. He did mention a ride. Fuck. I'm sorry Jon, I scream out into the blistering night. The drugs have left my body it feels, and again it (I) feel(s) cold.

Walking up and down san francisco's winding streets, unraveling and coming apart myself, I noticed how hard my heart was beating. I was sweating even though it was fairly cold outside. When I arrived at Jon's apartment, my bag was outside with a note attached to it. He must have been waiting for me to round the corner cause the bag was still there. I grabbed my bag and put the letter in my pocket. I looked up into his window, but the lights were off. I wished I had the strength to ring his doorbell. Wished I had strength.

I decided not to read the letter, ever. I would keep it, but couldn't accept losing anything else this week, especially not Jon. How could I have been so thoughtless? The cracks in the pavement hold me as I brave the strong wind, closing my jacket to fight back against the breeze. Now, I think, I am cold.

drink #3

It's been two months since I've talked to Jon. Two months since I decided to move in with Bryan, too. These two months hold a few different emotions for me. On one hand I am extremely happy with Bryan. I mean it is an unexpected blessing on my current situation. I had figured Jon's pad would have been my base, but I fucked that up royally, so there's that. And meeting up with Bryan and having everything be so easy, just makes the whole situation kind of odd, but hella cool. (PSA moment) It just takes a few weeks to begin using the old lingo from home, hella and hecka have attacked my reasonably broad, and intelligent vocabulary, but I'm hella cool with it.

I am working again.

It's a café job, but it is a job. You know 'not what I thought I was going to be doing', but it's what I am doing. At this time in my life I feel like it's cool. Bryan really doesn't want me to work here, but I told him I needed to make my own money and have, you know, my own life. And if I can be honest, I love my job! I have my own money and get to do what I love, all day. Smoke weed!

I thought I would read a lot at this café, but it gets fairly busy during the day. It's not just because the cappuccinos and espresso drinks are so good, but the café also serves as a medical marijuana dispensary. There is a constant stream of customers and ganja smoke all day long, streaming in and out of the doors. The bay area is the west coast's very own sunny Amsterdam on North American soil. Or, as I like to call it, Amsterdam by the bay, and the ocean.

Cannabis Doctors prescribe marijuana for various illnesses, and there are many people who come in the shop who have life threatening diseases, who are alive because of marijuana. I always said marijuana was medicine. And, of course there are people like me who believe in the preventative method - we like to smoke, so that we do not get sick.

Now, these doctors are very crucial to the system that provides marijuana for the clients who need this medicine. They, weed doctors, are not like the hospital kind because they actually care about their patients. You just tell them your ailment and they check off a list of possible strains of marijuana that can help you. You get your id card, and the rest is a smoky residue of love. It's the best doctor visit I've ever had.

Working in the café has been one of those experiences where everyday is completely different but invariably the same. The major constants are marijuana, of course, espresso, and cigarettes. Conversations range from illness to politics, to bush out of office, to sex, to marijuana laws, new shops opening up, the environment, and anything you could think of. But I'm always shocked when I hear the out of the world stories that you could never fathom, or have any reason to think about at all.

For instance, last week a man walked into the shop with a toupee on his chin. Now, I was like it's all good cause I know the bay area and anything goes with folks here. People are free to be whatever they want to be. It's what the Bay is known for, being completely free at all costs. But, there was something different about this guy. Cat made his purchase and then sat down for about an hour and half, just smoking and reading. He was reading a book on fetishes, which was normal as well. Then he picks up his weed from the table and puts it in his coat pocket, right. He walks back up toward me and says…

'Hey. I was thinking that I could pay you $150 dollars for about five minutes of work?'

'Five minutes?' I say

'Yay. I mean yes, just five minutes of your time sir.' He smiles and fidgets with his trouser pants.

I'm like, "Cool. That sounds cool. Doing what?"

"Do you have nice feet?" he says.

"What?"

"No offense, I'll just tell you what I want. I like feet, a lot. But, especially black men's feet. I feel like the darker the foot, the farther the distance walked. I'm fascinated by black men's feet and the journey their feet have endured. Many of my friends say that it's my white Jewish guilt, but I say it's passion. I love it; I mean them, feet. Where they've been. I'm turned on immensely by just looking at them. All you have to do is show me your feet while I masturbate, and I'll pay you. You don't have to touch me, and I won't touch you at all; I just want to look at your feet."

"This is not that kind of place." I say abruptly, constantly thinking about the $150 and what I could do it with it.

"Well, we don't have to talk about it here." He says sliding two bills folded up, a one hundred and a fifty.

My head is thinking about appearances and the fact that this man has a toupee on his chin, right? And then I think about what the hell he actually said. My feet? You just want to look? And he did say five minutes, right? Like, that's it? I say, I don't have to look at you or be too close, and he says no. So, $450 dollars later and a date for next week, I know the job is like only three minutes now, and he sits so far away in his big house that I couldn't see him if I tried.

My name is Frederic.

I am still staying at Bryan's house in Orinda. He was actually engaged to this Anglo-Saxon man from England for quite a long time. They bought this house together and everything just got crazy, and out of order. Bryan noticed that his boyfriend, I mean fiancé had a thing for black men. He noticed that their credit card had almost one thousand dollars of fees for Black porn. I think Bryan has always felt a little thing about not being 100% Black. I mean he is fine as fuck, but always feels he needs to play up how African he is, like it's his key to some kind of paradise. Shit, I love it, cause I love Black men, so fuck me nicka, fuck me, ya know? But for Bryan it was too much. He finally had to end it when he noticed how his insecurity about being mixed pushed his boyfriend even further away.

Bryan and I are not together, as far as logistics are concerned, and I think that is what makes it so great. Logistics. For me, the knowledge that I have an obligation to something makes it that much harder to fulfill. Like if I never say that it is there, then it's not. No tree, no forest, no fall, no sound. Remember that Dianetics shit, 'If a tree falls in a forest and no one is there, can you hear it?' I always answered yes you could hear the sound if nobody was in the forest, but now I know you can't hear shit, especially if you don't want to. Anyway, our schedules are so different, we barely see each other: he is either leaving when I am coming or vice-versa. It's actually the perfect situation. Cause when we see each other, it's magic. When we fuck, it's a kinetic participatory expression in black men fucking the shit out of each other. That's the best way to say it. (manny pacquia quickness::john coltrane smooth.)

My cell phone rings. It's my mother again. I answer this time, reluctantly. Radiohead's *Karma Hotel* blasts from the speakers.

"Hey Mama."

"Hey baby. You found a job yet? (without pause), Cause you know if you don't soon, I do not know what I'll do. What's that music I hear in the background? I want you to come home baby. Mama will take care of you. I know you say you're staying at that Bryan boy's house, but who is he anyway? Do you even really know him? Where is his family from? Baby, are you there?"

"Yeah. Mama, I am at work right now. Bryan is my friend. He is a brilliant man and has put your little boy up for the last two months. You know Jon dissed me. I've told you a million times that I do not affiliate with people who would make you embarrassed or shameful of me."

I smile to myself and make more fun at my mother's archaic beliefs, norms, and mores. I love when I can poke fun at my mother. I love her, but sometimes she surprises me with some of the things she says. I can remember when she worked as a waitress in a rock-and-roll nightclub and watching her do her thing always made me think she was the real rock star.

My mother had me young, and took me pretty much everywhere, even to her places of employment. I think I could repeat all of her jobs: shoe sales woman, bartender at (3) rock clubs in Chicago, a Director for six commercials, Producer on (3) scripts, and now a Professor at Columbia College for seven years in the film department. I may have forgotten something, but I was there, everywhere she was.

"Mom, I even take applications to see if I will play with people now."

"Boy, you know I do not have the time or the energy to listen to your foolishness, rudeness in some cultures. You know your mama only wants the best for you. I like for my baby to be on his best behavior and attune to his inner needs, and working. You know how we do. Our family comes from a long line of hard working Black people, baby. I'm just worried about you. Can a mama be worried about her baby in this new age of virtual reality? You got a job yet? Where are you anyway?"

"Mama, first of all I am twenty-five years old, and I have my B.A, and I am working, like I just said." I look up from the floor, kick a few espresso beans against the garbage can, and see a line of customers out the door.

"Hold on mama." Placing the phone down on the espresso machine.

"Can I take your order?"

"Let me get a cappuccino and an 1/8 of that purple haze." Mother's voice screams from cell phone, "What do you do baby? Baby? Can you hear me? I am talking to you."

My mother's voice trails off as I make an ugly face at the cell phone and prepare the cappuccino for the beautiful Black brother at the counter.

Dark chocolate, like me, medium build, beautiful eyes, hazel I think. As the cappuccino maker blasts my thoughts into space, I imagine the fine ass man in front of me in his underpants. The loud noise always sends me into my imagination. I think about the man at the counter, my mother's voice trailing off into cellphonelandia, and all the nasty things I could do to him. The steam, hot foamy islands of clouds, a trip in espresso-making wander takes my brain into the possibilities of sex, and I am almost at the point of climax, as the foam bubbles to froth. When his cappuccino is complete, I hold the cup with both hands to bring my hands to the temperature of my heart, slowly wiping the milk residue away. (I know I'm nasty.)

"So, here's your cap. Can I see your Medical Marijuana Card?" When I ask, I realize that my mother is still on the upside down phone screaming.

"I'm sorry sir, can you hold on for a minute."

"Sure," the beautiful man sings to me.

"Frederic, can you hear me?" My mother's voice sings or rings like a witch scratching her nails on a chalkboard in a classroom in hell.

"Mom, I will talk to you later!"

"Frederic, are you working at a café or something like that. I raised you better than that. I will not have a son of mine selling cappuccino, although your mother adores a good cappuccino, as well, I can't be having you selling purple coffee cakes either! You had me waiting on the phone while that loud espresso machine just had your mother's nerves ringing!"

My mother's voice is searing through metallic walls this time, and I am a little afraid to do what I know I have to do. The sexy man is looking at me with piercing, patient eyes, and I think I need to get off the phone with my mother right now and run off with him to some deserted island called his apartment.

"Mom, I have to go. I work at a medical marijuana café. I'm a doctor of medicine, kind of like an herbalist or a weed activist. I make espresso drinks, and I sell weed, okay! I'm doing a service to the world by enabling those with sickness to be healed. Did you know that California's soft criminalization of marijuana helps us use our tax dollars to fight actual crime on the street? And did you know that people who have various illnesses are better able to get help and be healed by the work that I do? Did you know that? Gotta Go - Peace sister. Two fingers. I'm out!"

I'm in deep shit, but I hang up the phone knowing that this is not the end of my mother's antics.

My mother is the kind of woman who always makes sense of her own nonsense. I have to give it to her though she raised me all by herself through her waitress jobs to her doctorate degree; she always had her baby with her. I guess that's the problem; I'm a 25 year old baby.
She's great and all, but sometimes I have to shorten the leash she has around my neck. I know she'll get at me when she can. She lives in Chicago, but that will not stop her from getting on a plane or sending my uncle over from Oakland to take a talking to me. I don't think she knows

that I am twenty-five years old and have been on my own since seventeen. I'm nearly at my mid-life crisis.

"I'm sorry man. That was my mom. She is a mess. She's a perfect mess, but a mess still the same. You know how moms can be?" I take a look at his card, and I get his name. "Thanks Akil." He looks at me, and I hand him his ID back. I think to myself that since I am still single and this man is so fine, I may have to….

"Hey, what's your name?" I hear him and think that maybe I should not respond. Maybe, I should retreat to my invisible self \the one who hides when confronted with the very thing he asked for in the first place. I smile and answer, "Frederic, pleased to meet you."

So, long story short, Akil turned out to be a debt that I almost was not able to pay. I caught gonorrhea from him, twice. Okay, I'll take responsibility for my stupid ass getting naked with his fine self, but fuck, damn, a STD?!!! Why your fine ass gotta have gonorrhea, and why I have to catch that shit twice? As if catching my first two venereal diseases in the same month was some sort of karma for some shit I did, in some past life, if not this one.

Anyway, after that my mother flew out two weeks later from Chicago, in a rampage and ended up staying for awhile. I was happy she came. She said she had a conference, but I know she wanted to make sure that I was still alive. Whenever she comes to San Francisco, it's a great opportunity to get some needed money and betterment on my life. When I was little I called my mother the provider. I don't know what or where that came from, but she made every situation better when she left it. I mean we went and had massages, facials, and three mud baths. She loves the W hotels, and I think she owns some stocks cause she is relentless in her dedication to the chain. Anyway, the time was good, and she fixed my bank account up a bit. And I look and feel quite amazing.

Hospital fixed my dick: Mama fixed my checking account. She wanted me to quit the café, and I understood why. I listened because she gave me more money than I would make in a whole year for just hanging out with her while she was at her conference. I know she tries. She even met Bryan and said she genuinely loved him, but didn't understand why someone that fine was gay. That made me upset and I asked her what she thought of me, was I not fine? We argued for a while, and she conceded like she always does by handing me her American Express card and running to her hotel room fake crying. It's a bit weird, but I always shop feeling really sad but buying loads of shit. My life is a bit mad, I know, but what am I suppose to do if not live it?

I thought it was wonderful that she came and met him since I was staying at the man's house. My mother was working on her beliefs about same sex relationships. She had an experience with a woman she was studying under, literally, when she was obtaining her doctorate degree. My mother surprised me when she told me this. I felt really close to her at that time and really felt like she confirmed my existence through her studies. But that was a short-lived bond. Even though she had a girlfriend she sometimes toiled with me about my same sex endeavors. I think she just likes to talk openly about the issues that she battles with on a daily basis and for some reason she feels like I am copying her or playing some kind of role to get attention. Sometimes I think she is right. I know I copy her when I drink a Greyhound, her favorite drink and mine too. The way she lights her cigarette at the beginning of a cocktail, and immediately at the end.

I rotate my wrist and allow the contents of the greyhound to bounce off of the ice cubes in my glass. I like the sound that it makes and the heaviness of the motion the glass makes in my hand. My cigarette sitting in the ashtray briefly, before I take my first sip. Sitting randomly at an anonymous bar tonight, actually wishing Bryan was not working, thinking that I just want to get high tonight.

I stop and take a sip from my drink. The drugs are kicking in and the alcohol too. I sit in the bar and think about the array of drugs I've done today. More time has passed and I am surviving off of the money my mother left me, and the donations from my toupee-bearded friend with the black male foot fetish. You got to be thankful for San Francisco. I have thought many days about what I am going to do about work, but since I have money right now I am not too worried about that. I hunger for the moment, and I thirst for its essence as I grab hold of life like a bird in flight holds unto the awaiting sky.

The winds have changed many times since the day my feet landed here. All of the faces and the feces that I've seen; all of the sentiments and saliva that I have swapped and swallowed. There seems to be a connection between the people that I have been sleeping with and meeting; the day-to-day bodily fluids that we all share in commonality, and my behavior. A natural relationship between the shedding of skin and the battle therein. These moments make everything clear. Like the reflection of ourselves in muddled water. Those moments when we are able to see ourselves clearly in the mud.

I stare at the people in the bar. Everyone seems to be smiling and having a good time. I end up alone most nights. Bryan and I have a late night affair. 'I'll meet ya at home' type of love. We like it like that. I finish my second drink and contemplate another. For some reason Akil pops into my head, and I shake the feeling off.

I motion at the bartender, but he doesn't see me. "Can I help you?" A man's voice, slightly familiar and sexy, asks from my blindsight.
It's Akil.

"I was just remembering you!" I say as I turn around violently in disbelief. "Where you come from?"

"I hope it was good, but I know it cannot be too good. You know, I'm sorry?" He says. His ass is still fine. Nasty as hell, but Akil is definitely fine as hell. I never knew why people weren't safe, especially me. I never thought I would ever catch something from anyone. But, that's what I get from sleeping with someone from the café. I always told myself not to mix work and sex, on any level. I mean I need to start mixing sex with condoms. I'm just happy I didn't give the disease to Bryan.

"Hey, you know I'm not mad at you. I just think you're nasty, and it's not good to not tell people you have a problem, you know, down there." Motioning to my dick.

"You're right. I guess I thought I could hide it from people. I just never really thought that shit was true what they said about those vd's. I mean we all made fun of people like that. I hope this does not sound too crass, but I figured since I did not have HIV, I was okay. But, I know now that I was stupid." Like watching the finest man in the world tell you he eats his toe-jam, or likes to eat other people's shit, this conversation was beyond ridiculous.

Okay, Akil was great looking. But, I just told you I caught the same disease from him twice. And, I am sitting here listening to him apologize to me for knowing he had funky dick and still fucking me twice, and I am still wanting to fuck him. What is it about good sex and big dicks that makes us, shit, makes my ass so stupid? I'm constantly exoticizing this man as he tells me about his dirty, nasty, stinky down there. Every word is not heard because I'm visualizing his naked ass fucking me, with a condom this time, but what the fuck! Do we sexualize ourselves so much that the fear of disease and the possibility of injuring our health are not important anymore? Is it like that Frederic? Am I so dick obsessed that I could endanger myself, and my partner, again? Shit, I have a partner now.

"You want another one? " Akil asks, and I say yes. My head is spinning now, kind of like a whirling dervish, but definitely without the religion.

I sit and talk to Akil for a bit and remember that he was a smart guy. He always had so much to say about everything. I also remember that he likes coke, so I hand him my stuff and wait for him at the bar while he goes to the bathroom. I think it would be nice to touch his lips and place my hand on his cheeks, feel his adam's apple with both my index fingers, and touch his nappy chest with my hands.

I think, I should just think about it.

Akil and I sit for a while, and I think it's time to go. I stand up but lose balance and fall flat on my back. I stand up making a scene, and Akil grabs me; I am saved from falling twice in the same club. We walk out together and for a minute I think maybe I could sleep with him, if I could construe what I was doing as thinking. I let Akil carry my weight and me to his car. The door opens, and I fall into the car. I collect myself and sit up. Thankfully Akil rolls the window down and the air from the Bay breeze holds me steady.

Black men. Myself. Distant. Idealized, romanticized and eroticized like Africa, like a dream, a diamond mind nightmare. My father a far off equation that never factored into the scenery of my childhood. Images flash back and forth, men running away and coming toward, staying for brief moments. Stopping. And going. Movement and stillness. Shades of myself reflected against mirrors facing windows, images escaping outside into the world, and unto the streets of the beckoning below. I watch myself on

broken television screens. It seems to be four hundred, a
television for each year of slavery. All broken in some way,
fractured images. Channels change rapidly, varying images
of myself being lynched, lurked and lusted after, loved and
learned, lessons left on skins and hearts of women and men
who have looked dark, dense blackness hard in the face of
reality. I reach out to myself and find a world of water,
running down centuries from the ocean tears of my heart.
Father was supposed to be close to these doors that I
opened when I touched William, Bryan, Akil. Mirrors of
ourselves in closed doors and under covers, exploiting the
over exploited black fallic, dangerously close to hanging or
gagging on images of myself with a dick in my mouth.
Black men, myself, distant and foreign, I look into the
mirror and reach out to touch myself in someone else'
arms, some man, someone who will take me. Even though I
know that I won't find my father in them, I still reach out
and hope for the end of this adventurous, but exhausting
search.

Akil drops me off at Bryan's pad. I walk up the stairs
holding on to the railings with all the strength I have left in
the world. Even my reserve energy is gone. It took
everything I had not to go home with him, but for some

reason I could not even fathom the idea of catching a third disease from the same person.

When I enter the apartment the smell of incense and marijuana permeate the space. I call for Bryan, but no one responds. I walk throughout the huge apartment and fall down in the hallway. My eyes close as I fall into a deep sleep for seven minutes. The phone rings, and I answer. It is Bryan. He is in Los Angeles, he says he tried to call me earlier, but my phone did not pick up. I check my calls and notice that he did call. I haven't looked at my phone all day. My head is pounding hard like I drank too much, or something. I can't even remember what I had to drink. I just knew I was safe from any more vd's. Hanging with fucking Akil had my mind all over the place.

"Okay, well what?" I say, a little annoyed, a lot drunk.

"I can get you a ticket if you want to meet me? I had no other choice Frederic. My work is moving fast and that's real good, right? More money and more travel, for both of us."

"Yeah, for sure. I'm a little tore up right now. Let's talk tomorrow, okay?"

"Okay, don't be mad at me. I can send for you tomorrow. I know we were supposed to meet tonight. Our nights are special Freddy-Mac…"

Bryan always does this. He makes me feel bad for not really giving a fuck where he is. I mean I would love to hold a clean dick like Bryan's tonight, but why would I get mad about you working? I mean, what? But, I don't say this cause I know I'll suck that, I mean we will see each other tomorrow.

What kind of money is Bryan making I think to myself in a haze. It seems like the men who I am attracted to the most are the ones who can take care of me. Give me the life that my mother gave me, without all the finger pointing and neck rolling.
"Bryan, you know I can't get mad at you, I'm just gonna miss you tonight in bed. I'll just take care of my drunk self real quick and fall into sleep. Don't get mad at me, I don't even know what I just said. I love you, and I'll talk to you soon."

"Tomorrow, baby, tomorrow." Bryan yells as I hang up the phone and lie down in the middle of the hallway floor. My head is aching, and the pain is seething. You ever think of the pain the earth went through during the tectonic shift? My head feels like it is separating into new continents, forming new land, splitting into parts that seem foreign. Seem to be taking parts of me here, and other parts there, like I may have done too many drugs, drank too many grapefruit juice and vodkas. I try and close my eyes and think of peaceful things, but all I hear is loud crashing waves, smashing against the peace I'm trying to conjure.

My eyes are closed, and sleep finally lays me flat like a bulldozer. My headache meshes into blackness. If I was not breathing I'd probably be dead. My body is sprawled between the bathroom floor and the bedroom. My clothes still on, cell phone in hand, and consciousness long gone.

I fall, like Alice, down a deep hole. Without all the talking animals and mad hatters. Without the growing taller, and the growing smaller. Without the pomp and circumstances of a children's novel.

As I black out I begin to dream. Like I am conscious, everything very clear, like a glass of water that I should have drank before I fell to the floor. This dream feels real, almost too real. It scratches like a broken record, and I'm

back at the bar with Akil, but we're in NYC?

I'm back at the bar with Akil, but we're in NYC?

a bar with Akil,

but in NYC,

in NYC?

Akil?

(a dream.)

drink# 4 DREAM SEQUENCE:

Frederic is still lying sprawled in the hallway, half of his seemingly broken body is in Bryan's bedroom, and the other is in the bathroom. As if the dream is being televised and you, the reader, are watching it on a small television, each bold segment is another channel the television changes for you to watch. Enjoy.

WELCOME TO THE DREAM:
(In NYC)

Akil asks if I want another; I respond, **1** more greyhound for the road. I end up drinking **2** more greyhounds and leave with him. We walk together down Christopher St. in the Village, holding hands and kissing passionately. Bryan calls **3** times, and I don't answer. My head starts spinning, and I throw up **4** times. Akil holds me so I don't fall into the messy pavement. Although I leave with Akil, I do not sleep with Akil; even in my dream, I am not stupid. I catch the number **5** bus to **6**th avenue and walk home to see if Bryan is still up. Now, it seems that I am back in San Francisco… and I'm running and singing out loud the whole way. It's **7**o'clock in the morning, but I know Bryan.

I ring the bell and Bryan answers in his sweat-pants-no-shirt-outfit. It's most sexy, but he is not smiling. He is standing in the doorway, and I see a foot in the background. I wonder whose foot that is. The man moves to grab a blanket, and I see that it is Akil. Our eyes meet. My smiles fall to the ground, and I catch them while spitting **8** times in Bryan's face. He hits me in the nose, the eyes twice, the head four times, and twice in the back, **9** times in all. I'm out for the count. One, two, three, four, cinco, six, sept, huit, nine, **10**.

a voice speaks on mega-phone

"I heard that Sonia came and picked me up, and I heard that Sonia took care of me for like a week and a half. I heard she came cause Bryan called her cause he was gonna kill me. I also heard he told her to come and get me, or he would call the police or kick my ass some more. Said I started some shit at the house and he had to kick my ass. Said that we wasn't even together as a couple. Something about logistics and that I had suggested we don't be a couple, and when he was fucking someone else, I walked in and acted like an asshole. I don't remember that? He said something about me that I had created some stupid story in my dumb ass little black head. He actually called me dumb and little. Said if he wanted to sleep with Akil he could. It wasn't like he knew him. Said the guy said his name was Sergio. Said he just met this guy after he got off work, and since I was in New York he thought he could do whatever he wanted to do. But, I thought **I** was in New York with Akil? Wasn't I?

Cut to Sonia's house

"Frederic, you got your ass kicked very badly and we are going to have to do some tests. I think you should try and get some rest."

"Sonia, why are you talking like a nurse?"

"I am a nurse, stupid."

My ass was really hurting. I felt fucked up. All over my body sang a Death Metal song, each ball and joint finding itself impossibly not functioning. I couldn't remember what happened and why Sonia was talking like a nurse. I wanted to find out what happened with Bryan. Was he still mad with me? Why was he with Akil? Knowing Bryan, he probably wouldn't get so mad that he would never speak with me. I started feeling better. Where was I? I looked around the hospital and realized that I was still in Sonia's house.

"Sonia!" I screamed.

"What the fuck, boy, you alive, huh..?" Sonia appears out of thin air, standing by the door.

"I just started to think that I was feeling better and wanted to know about Bryan."

"If you start talking that shit about Bryan right now I'll kick ya ass too. You ain't been nothing but trouble for Bryan since you got back here, and I'm sorry ... I'm sorry, I think you need to deal with your shit and deal with them kids and that school system that fucked you up! You have never actually dealt with that situation at all Freddie. Hell, you were on fucking CNN. Papers in major cities around the country had your fucking name in em. You were at one point in time fighting for some cause, now you just sit here, and there, and come and go, can't really hold a job. I mean I don't want to sound harsh man, but fuck, what are you even doing here?

Your friends have always loved you. Why we have to pay for some shit we did not do, when the people who did this, is still fucking you!"

Her words send me to a **high school:**

screaming children running, bleeding. hands reach out and oceans separate the children from their screams. they drown. cameras are pointed at me from every angle.

I watch from the shore of a beach. I run out into the cold lake Michigan water, until the water covers my head. Like swimming against the current. The water rushes in and devours my lungs.

San Francisco, Tenderloin area.
Walking down empty streets looking through windows and open doors, my stomach is rumbling and my head pounding. Coffee bean fragrances meander through my erratic thoughts and become the present moment's engagement. Dancing through the dew that formulates on

green blades of grass in the park. I take off my shoes and feel nerves in my feet that I never knew existed. Currents are wet; electricity sparks new consequences, producing energy in far away spaces. I light the pipe. The lighter burns my thumb again. It is always black now. Smoke fumes exhale from my lungs, and I place my hand on the cold concrete to embrace my fall. I fly through the sky, and blue hues collect and form shapes in the clouds. I am rigid in my imaginings. Life after life, becoming anew, a variation on what was, and a critical analysis of what is happening right now. An opinion is stated, agreed as truth in the mind of the believe_r. And all things are safe in my head again. As long as I believe that there is peace happening here, then there is peace.

I have not returned to Bryan's house in three weeks. The last month could kiss my ass. I lost my phone at that party where I got beat up. I think it was a party. I kind of lost a lot at that party, but I cannot truly remember that much else, only that some important things were lost. I don't even know if it was a party. I keep being told by the mirror and wide-eyed stares of people passing by that something is lost.

I am sitting on the sidewalk now.

People walk past me and thoughts run along with the heels of passer-bys shoes. I'm taken to a memory of seeing shoes and pants legs, women's stockings and the edges of dresses. Sitting near my grandma's feet in her parlor as older ancestors' funerals occur. One funeral after another. I saw a lot of dead bodies as a child. And a lot of shoes.

I cannot quite remember why I am not at Bryan's house; have I run away? Where is Bryan anyway. Has he run away? All I can say is that I forgot to remember the details.

I am staring at the ground. My hand is bleeding. Scenes of my life appear in between the cracks of the concrete. Not my whole life but the last three weeks that seem to have led me to this corner of…. "where am I?"

The **first scene** seems to be in Bryan's apartment/

Bryan is not inside of his apartment. No one is inside of the apartment, and the oven is on. At least it seems to be no one there. The scene is shot from the vantage point of one of the ghosts of Christmas past**present**future in the christmas carol, and I am like one of the ghost leading myself, I guess, hovering above what seems to be the past?

I fly room to room, until I notice his bedroom is trashed. As if someone broke into his place. The television is turned upside down, and the glass from the coffee table is broken in tiny bits on the orange shag carpet. Why is the oven on? As I fly through the bedroom I notice Bryan's body naked on the floor with a pipe in his hand, half of his body is in the bathroom, his legs extend into his/our bedroom. I close my eyes. He is not moving. He is still. Is he dead/
fade to black.

scene 2

The door opens and shuts, and I see myself running out of the apartment. Is this the same day? I run through a neighbor's back yard and hide in the alley. I sit still in the alley until I fall asleep.

Everything is moving really fast right now like a Beyonce or Puff Daddy video, and I need someone to talk to. What happened to Bryan? I scream out loud, over and over again.

People pass me by, and I must be one of those crazy people asking strangers where Bryan is - when they don't know either one of us. I attempt to grab this woman's attention, and her boyfriend hits me in my mouth; I fall to the ground. I struggle to my feet.

"Where is Bryan?" "What happened to Bryan?" "Who the fuck are you?" The questions spit from my mouth, my pipe falls, I crumble down with each piece of glass. The stars dim to a sudden darkness and will never shine again, at least not the same brightness. People walk over me this time as I lie face down in the concrete.

Static.
White noise.

A little boy sits atop a hardtop orange 1971 Volkswagon Karmini Ghia. He wears a plaid blue and red flannel shirt and bright red corduroys. The boy carries a yellow megaphone and screams out the details of the next chapter of Frederic's dream. His smile is as bright and loud as his little voice coming from the mega-phone.

@1979 Weibolt's Department store, Evanston, IL..
"Frederic." A short, pregnant woman says as she rubs her stomach, staring deeply into a store mirror. Her cocoa skin

shining in the mirror's reflective stillness, the innocence of her eyes detail her youth.

"You are my precious baby. I love you so much Frederic. That's what I am going to name you. It's so French, and I love French class, and my teacher Monsieur LaBlanc. I want you to always remember that you can do anything. Even before you come out and into this world I want you to know some very important things. I want to start telling you this now because it's hard for a black man out here Frederic, and you gone be a black man one day. I want you to always know that greatness is your reward." The woman rubs her stomach looking at herself in the mirror, her eyes are direct, full of contemplation and anticipation. Her reflection is stunning because of the light in her eyes, and her abnormal shape for a girl her age.

"Can I help you?" a sales clerk appears in the corner of the mirror.
"Oh, I'm sorry, I was just thinking out loud... to my little man." She slowly moves out from the mirror, patting her stomach. "I think I want to get this dress and this sweater. I'm not so into these pants, however. Thank you."

"Okay, this way." The woman leads her from the mirror. Empty, the mirror's static image of colorful clothes on varying racks, lingers.

@1988 Robert Greenspan's house, Evanston, IL.

"Frederic, leave me alone!" Boy pushing hard against door. "Mom, Frederic is trying to get in my room! I'm trying to change my clothes. I don't have any clothes on!"

"Frederic, where are you? Are you pushing against Robert's door?"

"No, Mrs. Greenspan." Frederic voice trails off as he responds, pushing harder against Robert's door. When the door opens, Robert is standing, panting and out of breath. Robert is in his underwear. A nine-year old Frederic stands in the open door way, his mouth open wide like door, penis slightly erect.

@1993 Evanston Township High School, (ETHS) Evanston, IL..

"Frederic, I dare you to fuck Janet!" Billy screams out loud. In front of Janet and in front of the entire algebra class, the question rings like the lunch bell, drowning out the screams of excitement from the loud anticipating youth. "Yea,

Frederic, I dare you." Janet adds in sucking on her pen's cap. Frederic stands up in the middle of class, teacher's back to students, grabs Janet, and starts to French kiss her to the class's rants and screams.

@1993 ETHS

"Frederic, you are under arrest. Put your hands behind your back, son."

@1993 ETHS

"Frederic tried to put his hands on my dick!"

"What?" Frederic's voice is timid; a sense of guilt resides in his question.

"Yes, he tried to get me when I fell asleep, and he will admit it."

"Frederic, did you grab Berry's penis?" Mr. Willis, the Health teacher asks. For some reason it felt fitting that Mr. Willis would ask me about another boy's penis. Mr. Willis' penis was always on my mind, I guess because it seemed to be always hard, even now.

"Uh, no?"

"Frederic, it's okay to be gay or to like boys. I know you are still young and trying to figure it all out, but I want you to know that it is okay for boys to like boys."

"Uhhhh, nasty." Frederic and Berry both say in unison.

@ 1997 University of Illinois, Champaign, Urbana IL.

"Frederic, hold me."

"I don't want to."

"Please, we can say we were drunk, just put your hand in my pants and hold me." Directing Frederic's hand down his pants, Andre holds tight unto Frederic's waist. Frederic's hand grabs a hard Andre and begins to feel himself getting bigger in his levi's jeans.

"Oh."

"I told you, you would like this."

"You never said that. And I never said I liked it."

"You don't have to, your big dick is doing all the talking. Do you mind if I just lay here and hold you all night?" Andre's voice rings in Frederic's ears as he falls asleep, hand firmly in Andre's pants, holding onto Andre's penis-shaped rock.

@2000 Velvet Lounge, Chicago, Illinois

"Frederic…This is my friend William. William, this is Frederic." A woman with big hair and wide smile introduces Frederic and William. Both men salute each other, but have met just minutes prior in the bathroom line of the jazz club.

@2002 Frederic's apartment, Chicago, Illinois

"Frederic, I aint shit, and you aint shit. We just two black men, jack. What the fuck we look like, two black men fucking and shit. I mean what we gon' do raise kids and shit like that? That's a joke, we can barely stand each other sometimes. (silence) I think the best thing for you to do is to leave me right now. I know we just met and the shit has been real good, but I'll probably leave you in the end. Like some tragic movie, we will both not ever want to see. Some dramatic exit, somewhere in Brasil or something beautifully sardonic like that. (long pause) What a shame it will be. You will feel so betrayed, and I will feel redeemed because, of course from my perspective, I had been the one doing all of the work. The beautiful maiden who has her heart open and willing, but to the wrong man in the end. Maybe I will feel like I had been working the hardest to make you happy. But, you'll say fuck me and it's okay, we probably will fuck and then part for a while and still get together from time to time, even fall in love and shit again. But I'm telling you, leave me now. Forever. I just know I don't believe in this kind of love. I want to. I've always been attracted to men and always wanted to know what it was like to have someone really touch me. Hold me and feel me like I feel myself. I know I want a man's hands on my body. Your hands! I know it's you I am supposed to be in love with, but I can't do it. I know now, and I want you to know this before we both get hurt."

hospital_present (dream) time
(from vantage point of someone [Frederic] watching television in an reclining easy chair.)

day one

The white light in hospitals against the white walls define antiseptic and sterile, both. As well, the whiteness also reminds you of what they say it looks like when you pass over, or in some cases pass back by again. I feel like I passed over, maybe came back into the living for a reason, huh?

The nurse looks into my face like I look a bit scary, and I believe her, so I ask for a mirror. But, I can't say mirror, and she leaves without paying my mumblings any attention. I feel a bit weird, like, I feel good. They must have given me loads of drugs, cause there is no pain. And at the very least I am alive. It's just I cannot speak. When I realize this I feel more calm and relaxed. I figure I'm in a hospital, and someone will tell me what's wrong with me eventually. I keep asking myself why I am here and reach to scratch my head, pulling hard against my wrist and the bed frame; handcuffs nearly snap my wrist off. My wrists were in handcuffs, both of them. This is something. Why is this so familiar? I stare into the white wall, reality, a 40 ft Mack truck races after me. I see myself in handcuffs being led off out of the back of a building. The building looks like some institution of some kind, a school. My school. Me teacher. ARRESTED. I'm screaming obscenities and fighting the police officers back, restrained by the handcuffs but still fighting. There are like 1,000 young people watching me in the background, the noisy backdrop to this madness. I realize that we are in a high school. I am being arrested. I have handcuffs on my wrists. I've been here before. The young people watching are students at the high school. I am being pulled out, screaming. I begin to sing Bob Marley's *buffalo soldier* real loud and really off key. "dred lock rasta, in the land of America, fighting on arrival, fighting for survival. Stolen from Africa, fighting on arrival." I watch myself being taken from the school campus and thrown into a paddy wagon. Inside of the paddy wagon, I cry blood tears, ravaged by the consequence of this injustice.

Inside these four white walls, enclosing me and freeing me simultaneously, I am crying because I remember. I am not afraid to remember, again. I know that this is not why I have handcuffs on now, but that does not matter to me. The only thing that matters is the realization that I am remembering that thing, that oppressed feeling that stopped my progression, at least stopped it in my head. Knocked me out cold, Mike Tyson style. Feels like the situation got me here, doing all these drugs and fucking up everybody's life, especially my own. Right now, I feel the moment of clarity so to speak; my eyes are opening wide. No longer eyes wide shut but fucking piercing light. When everything, as fucked up as it was, becomes, finally, crystal clear.

The fact that I was a black man was clear. The fact that black men get arrested was also clear. The fact that I was a teacher and still, since I was a black man, I could be arrested in school was clear. I was face to face with the stereotype of myself. It's actually more like back to back, like in those westerns when people would draw their pistols and shoot to the death. We both have guns, the stereotype of myself, and my real self, we begin to take the five steps before we both must turn and fire, probably killing each other. When the count reaches five, we both turn to face each other and aim, but I scream loud breaking the plexiglass barrier of remembering, and this reality of being handcuffed to the hospital bed. I enter a place of awareness, instead of dying by my own hands. Face to face with an awareness of myself that I have never fully known, I close my eyes.

day #2

in the hospital

(or at least second conscious day. Awake.)

Well, this is the situation I learned today from the attending nurse. I was on the streets fighting random people when I was arrested. Supposedly I was screaming at these poor people because they were going to work, and they were out with their families shopping, or whatever I felt they were doing that was not right.

I mean a small part of me laughs when the nurse explains why I am in handcuffs. The police claim that I was ranting about how bad I thought the **Go-Go's** were as a group and allegedly, I flicked them off from time to time. Remember that group, the **Go-Go's?** The nurse explained that I spit in someone's face, and a sea of memories rushed over me. This time I wished I only had a headache. I close my eyes again and forget to think about everything I remembered. I fall asleep.

(still in dream)

When I am released from the hospital, I walk aimlessly until I find a school where I can write in my journal. Being sober has revealed a world without everything I thought I had when I came back to San Francisco. Even some valuable aspects that I never thought I would lose. Bottom. I have hit my own personal hell - fuck hitting BOTTOM. When I try to sleep it feels like I do a good job of trying, but when I look at the clock, I realize that I have only slept for four to seven minutes. You know how fucking crazy that is to sleep for no time and feel like it has been a long time? Annoying.

I rock back and forth, like a baby in fetal position. Sucking my thumb and staring into the open window, I notice the grey of the clouds never leave. Each day I awake and lay rest to a desolate sky, my screams like a hound in the country, howling forever. It feels so sad to remember what has all transpired in the short months since I have returned to San Francisco. It's funny, when you begin running from things, you end up running head first back into the brick wall you built to forget about what you were running from in the first place. It's like we are always running back to that place that we buried so deep down inside. We manifest it again and again and again. I have been running so hard to get here. Immobile and unable to shut out these thoughts. I lie in fetal position to remember what it must have been like when I was a baby and mama rocked me to sleep instead of these shakes and fits, wearing me out physically. The night sky, with all her secrets agrees to play mother tonight. She covers me simply in the mystery of a possible morrow.

dream sequence ends. Thank you reader. The dream is now over. The television set is now black. Frederic is sprawled on the floor of Bryan's house. He was out drinking with Akil, got drunk and was smart enough not to sleep with Akil. Again. Instead he was asleep dreaming.

Violently I wake and wipe the sleep out of my eyes. A cold sweat, body shivering and eyes as big as saucers, I touch my face to make sure I am indeed awake, alive for that fact. "How long have I been asleep? Where am I? What the fuck was all of that?" The scenes from the dream play over and over in my head. Fear seeps into me, and I am afraid of what would have happened if I did not wake up. Everything that I can remember frightens me, and everything I forgot seems to be that way for safety. For a minute I think I need to get things together; I need to clear my head somehow. I've never had a dream like that before. It felt like seven or eight segments of some horrendous shit. Something like a warning, something like a searing pain that I fear will never leave me. My eyes hurt, and my body is spinning. Or is it that my body hurts, and my head is spinning?

I try and find myself, waking up I look around and realize that I am at Bryan's apartment. **That dream was fucked up.** It felt like I was asleep for days. I grab my phone, and it is dead on the floor next to me. I walk toward the window, pull open the shades and see the dark night reflecting back at me. It is nighttime. Damn, I must have slept through the whole day. I plug my phone into the wall and charge it. I pick up Bryan's house phone and call my number to hear my messages. The first three messages are from Bryan wondering where I am, and why my phone is off. At least he is not dead, I say. I keep having images from the dream interrupting my new sense of wakefulness. The next message is from Akil. It is sweet, but very strange. He said that he wanted to meet up with me tonight, said he wanted to tell me something. I immediately erase his message and call Bryan back.

"Hey." His voice is weathered, and Bryan sounds a bit out of it. Still a comfort to hear. "What's up?"
"Nothing much. I just woke up."
"From last night?"
"Yes. That shit is crazy as hell Bryan. I had the craziest dream that I have ever had. There were so many crazy things in that dream. I can't even begin to talk about it because it was so scary, not just scary but like my whole life. I'll tell ya later. Is that ticket still open for me? I really need to get away."
"I'm sending you a ticket for tomorrow. I mean I had one for you for today, but obviously that won't happen. I'll just change it with the agent after we finish talking. How about four o'clock tomorrow? Is that okay?"

Bryan asks, and I laugh cause that is all I want from him, a way out of this craziness; a new scenario. Even if it is Los Angeles, my old stomping ground.

We talk for a while, and I hang up.

I walk into the bathroom and stare in the mirror at myself. I wash my face with cold water and glimpses of insight. My eyes are red and blaring forth an idea of what it all must mean. I stare at myself for a while longer and walk into the kitchen. Looking through the refrigerator, I find some grapefruit juice. I search through the cabinets to find some vodka. I find the Absolut and notice that it is only a corner left. I pour out some grapefruit juice and add the remainder of the vodka. I add some ice and leave my drink on the coffee table near the television. I pick up the remote control, but put it back down. I stare into the dead television set and see my image. Mirror, mirror on call, who's the most beautifullest of them all??

I am awake.

I light a cigarette and close my eyes.

drink_#5

In the morning Bryan calls. His voice is rustic and long lost
cousin, sentimental and lethargic all in equal timing. I offer
to take the greyhound to Los Angeles for nostalgia's sake,
both Bryan and I laugh. My flight leaves at four o'clock out
of San Francisco International Airport. Bryan makes me
promise that I won't be late, definitely not miss the flight
this time. I promise. Bryan blows kisses good-bye while
my penis hardens, and the phone goes silent.

My body feels rested since I slept two whole days. I hadn't
felt this good in a long time. I take a shower, get dressed,
and take a train to my favorite café in San Francisco, near
Sonia's house.

"Can I get this new york times and a pack of dunhill
international lights? The red package, yea, that one. A
cappuccino as well, and, uh, a lighter." Cigarette and
lighter appear as shopkeeper moves swiftly to the espresso
machine.

The older gentlemen at the café never remembers anyone who comes in, no morning hello, no smile, just precise questions about what you buy. I light a dunhill.

"You read the times?" he says to me handing me my cappuccino.
"Yeah sometimes." I reply reading the times.
"No smoking inside." He hands me my change.
"I know that's why I'm leaving." My feet feel the heat of the sun first and then the rest of my body is immersed in sunlight.

I grab an empty table near the edge of the terrace. The café is bustling, and the sun seems to be dancing off of the faces of everyone. Like a garden of people, everyone seems to be uniquely placed in this array of wisdom seekers, dreamers, artists and thinkers, just like dandelions, roses, and lilies. West Coast Bohemians and other superheroes like me engage in coffeeshop talk: politics, save the whales, green the earth, feed the children, impeach the man, honor thy woman, rear thy child, talk, talk, talk. Guess that's why I love the coffeeshop so much. The petty bourgeoises' Parliament or House of Representatives.

When my skin realizes how hot it is, I make a frightening discovery. It's like I haven't seen the sun in a long time. Every morning starts around 4 p.m. for me. My nights begin at 11 p.m., littered with drug infused nights, good sex, really good sex actually, but late starts to new days. It's crazy that I'm up this early. I got to get my shit together I think to myself, and stare hungrily into the blue sky for an answer, at least acceptance.

My cell phone rings. **"RESTRICTED"** flashes on the LCD screen. Let me tell you my philosophy on **"RESTRICTED"** appearing on my cell phone. **"RESTRICTED"** usually signified one of three things for me. The call is, either a booty call, a bill collector or one of my old lovers who knows I wouldn't answer the phone if his or her muthafuckin' name appeared. It's basically a game of Russsian Roulette, anyone of these calls could be the bullet that kills me.

"Hello." I hear myself answer, annoyed, but curious.
"Hey babe. How are you?"

Like an avalanche on a mountain high, a sun-pierced blue sky, something like my heart falls from these heights, tumbling to a hard-surface-ground, crashing through thick webs of my own inner confusion. It is William's voice, and I know I am not going to hang up on him even though I should. Even though I don't even know my name right now, even though I can't remember to be angry anymore.

"Babe? Who is this?" I pretend I don't recognize this voice. "Don't play. Why you acting like you don't remember me, and this voice? Stop acting like you don't know me anymore. (silence) You don't know me Frederic? It's been that long?" William's voice, familiar as my own, even more because of all of the whispering into my ears, and the stories we'd share of where we were from and where we'd go – together, we had always said. William always had a way of coming back, and I always had a way of welcoming him, even though I knew I shouldn't.

"Of course, I know who this is. I know everything about you - baby. It just sounded so weird to hear you say baby, when you don't really think I'm your baby do you? I mean where are you? France, Belgium, Senegal, Mars? We've been so far away, and I've had to follow your career by reading the paper. I knew you were back in the States, living in New York, but I had to read that shit in the

fucking newspaper William!" When I hear myself
screaming I realize immediately that I am angry.

*william never will be erased from my head, my body; each
finger and each toe, my lips, hips, shoulders and penis
knows his name, my back, chest, arms, and knees have a
memory of him that will forever be tattooed. They too know
his name well. my skin: sacred spaces written out in his
language, inscribed inside my eyelids is his profile, his
arms, head, ass, back, chest, hands, and toes, his black
skin, his hand on my hand. on my tongue his tongue rests,
laying together, comforter and blanket in winter winds. she
is my man, he is. this woman that exists within us, our
mothers' creation-male, we are black men loving, harder
than ever; i am dreaming while awake. standing up while
seated. immersed again in your insanity, William, i am
listening to you. naked. feet in shallow water, answering
your call William.*

"I'm living in the east village right now and moving to a
loft in Brooklyn in forte green at the come of the new year.
You have to come out when I go home. I got a special room
for you. (silence) But that is not where I am right now, at
least not physically; I'm actually much closer to you.

(silence) I'm in Los Angeles, and I want to see you. I can send you a ticket and some money for you to get here? Can I send for you Frederic?"

Can you imagine what is going through my head? My poor head, just a few moments ago I thought I was doing okay, thought I had my shit together. I mean survived that fucking dream. Now, I was headed to Los Angeles to be with my current boyfriend that by the way has been laying it down, both literally and figuratively. I mean I'm on my way to LA First Class and with a limousine driver awaiting me. (I don't even believe that.) This muthafucka calls at the height of my happiness and I'm stuck on stupid, yet again actually contemplating seeing William again. I'm going to see William again. Fuck contemplate! The fucking record is scratched; I'm going to see William again.
See William again
William
Again.

"William. I don't know what to say. (I take a brief pause to quickly pull out a cigarette and light it.) Why don't you just put the money in my account, and I'll be there tomorrow; it's the same account number." Each drag from the cigarette reminds me of why I know I am going to see William this weekend. Even, if I have to lie to Bryan.

"Yup, that's my babe. Think with your heart, and soon I'll be able to hold you in my arms again. Rub my fingers through your hair, if you even have any hair now. I just want to hold you again Frederic. (pause) So, cool. That's what I'm going to do. I'll put $500 in your account. And, I'll see you this weekend? (pause) Frederic? (pause) You know Frederic I'll always love you, even though I've never known how to love you. I know this sounds so weird coming out from thin air, but I know you've been thinking about me like I've been thinking about you. All the time, man. I mean I can't get you off of my mind. I just know now that I made a mistake. We all make mistakes, a lot of them, and sometimes I wish I could rewind my own life and make more sense of things, but I know I cannot.

And you know, Frederic, I know that I have said some awful things to you, my black brother, and it is time for some sort of healing, apology, something. I think sometimes, that all of this is some kind of horrible joke. You know the mad emotions that I feel for you and all the wonderful times we have shared and the life we have lived together. But still it has no validation in the outside world. You sit back and sometimes feel so alternative that you do not even know how to analyze yourself because you don't know the fucking criteria. You know what I mean? Like you have to create all of that too! Yourself and the criteria for evaluating that self! You know, like you learn all of this bull shit that isn't applicable to your "real" life, and when it comes down to creating the person that you want to be, you realize that all that you learned growing up about right and wrong, and mores and norms was just constructed concoctions, which at the same time were false, but have extremely real consequences."

"You know, you say some interesting things, 'my brother'. I do not know if I or we should get this deep this early in the morning. Maybe I can reply to something that you said about all of this "kind of" coming out of thin air. This is not kind of *'like coming out from thin air Will',* this is fucking coming from 'I don't even know where?' I have not spoken to you since you left the country the day I arrived to Los Angeles. (silence) Do you remember that at all? Did you know I was coming there to live with you William? Remember you invited me? (silence) You don't have to say nothing. I will always love you too. And that's the problem.

Forever and ever like a fool loves his master. And it gets sicker when you think about how much the master, ultimately, loves his slave. I know that analogy is fucked up, but so is this situation we're in right now. Like, I'm definitely going to come out there and see you, and, that is the very thing that I don't need to do, but I know I will. I'm standing real close to the yellow line at the subway, leaning comfortably toward the approaching train, leaning toward you."

"Frederic, I just want to hug you again. Kiss you and feel your heartbeat against mine again. You know I love you baby. I'm destined to you, my beautiful Frederic. Let's talk when you get here, face to face. I'm online right now, and the money will be there soon."

Like nothing ever changed. William calls, and I respond. Hands me some money, makes me feel good about me and I'm his, even when he hurt me like no one has ever done. I hang up the phone and light another dunhill; inhale, exhale, sip the foam-crested cappuccino, add more sugar, and repeat, inhale, exhale, sip the foam-crested cappuccino, inhale, exhale - and continue with william, continue smoking dunhill, continue fucking william..

Images of war on the cover of the nytimes, a president from some country declaring more war on another country. Something about defending democracy and the importance of fighting the recent election conspiracy in his country is declared by another "leader" of the world. I place the folded war, its excuses and declarations on the table and put my glasses on to block the glaring sun.

Rummaging through the contents of my mind I start to remember certain elements of that dream. Most of the time, my dreams are fairly intense, but this one was a bit overwhelming. I've tried to write it down to document it, but I've lost most of what happened in my subconscious. I'm scared to look at the dream too literally. To stop and look at what the consequences of my actions could actually lead to.

I can't stop seeing the young faces, scared and running away from angry police officers forcefully re-directing the young people with guns drawn. A lineage of pain, inherited, worn like indigenous tattoos, sacred scars we hold up to the light, sharing with each other how much it really didn't hurt. I just don't have the time right now to deal with issues that I've buried inside. I'd rather keep them locked up instead of unleashing the avalanche and being buried in my own shit. I'm running straight till the lights go out, not looking back, taking no prisoners.

Aren't dreams just spaces in our mind where thoughts and ideas that we have not lived out in our consciousness spill out and into our subconscious, littering that deep dark space with swallowed fears, insecurities, and lost loves? As if, we live parallel lives through our dreams. Some things have to come to the light, right?

I am stuck with the words that dream-William spoke. That old conversation that made me want to kill him. All his talk of black love between two men not being possible, or real, made me think that maybe he was right. The inevitability of black men falling together to the pit of hell for this un-sanctified love as the only possible result of the union. I just think it's so unoriginal and *like* not true, and when William said that shit, I knew he was hurting and wanting me to hurt too. And for a co-dependent ass like me he was perfect. I took what he said and made sure that I proved to him everyway I could that he was wrong, and we could be in love together without the curse he placed on homosexuality.

All the times he said he loved me. Shit, all the times everybody said they loved me. What me did they love? Could the "me" that they loved so much not receive that same love when they really found out who I am? Would they still love me?

Love.

Love can heal everything. Love can save the world. Love can kiss my ass. Cause, every time I think I'm in love, it just means that I am at the point where I will let someone else's desires take precedence over my feelings. Can I help you? You need something baby? I got you - you know I got you; but who got me?

Damn, what am I going to do? What the fuck am I even doing thinking about any of this? All of this sounds so crazy. He sounds like such an ass. I know I want to see William, but Bryan is there too. And I think I am in love with both of them. At least, I know I am in love with Bryan. And I could use a good William fuck. That sounds crass, I know. Base even. But, throughout it all, I guess I'm still curious about William.

My phone rings again, and this time it is Sonia. Her voice is a welcomed interruption from my own inner dialogue about how bad I am going to feel once William and I have sex a few times. Feels like I have not spoken with Sonia in a long time. The last we spoke it was in the dream.

"What's up girl?"

"Hey Fredric, what you doing?" (My whole name swimming in her mouth sounds chilly.)

"I'm at the café near your house. On my way to LA to see him and William." My laugher is met by silence. "Are you still there, Sonia?"

"Freddie, are you crazy? I mean, I thought you gave up on William? He ain't right for you man, I just feel like that night we spent together when you first got here was a freeing of all of that shit for you."

Sonia's voice is warm again and welcoming, and I know she means well, but something about how she says you and me makes me feel her own neediness.

"Sonia, don't go there, please. The night we spent and all of the nights we have spent are freeing to my soul and my being, but that does not do anything to free up the space that always will love him. I just feel like I cannot do anything when he calls but to answer."

"What if that muthafucka is still a muthafucka and you get there, fuck up Bryan's perception of you, and then Will plays the shit out of you again. I do *not* think I could handle that story. I just want you to be happy."

"I know, but what does that mean anyway, happiness? I think about William and I get so happy at times, it is like the weather, right. The Bay area weather. It is never predictable, but it is always expected, but what becomes important is how well we are prepared for the unexpected."

"Whatever baby, I'm on my way over there. Now, order me a cappuccino with extra foam. Is that cute waiter over there? No matter, I'll see ya in a minute."

I hang up the phone and think about what Sonia just said. William would not dare leave me again, would he? Damn, this shit sucks. I just want someone to love me. I don't have time for all of this mess.

Since Sonia thinks she knows everything I call my bank to check if the money is there from William, and I'm relieved to hear that it is there. I take a sigh of relief and think Sonia has no idea who William really is and who I am for that matter. I know it is hard to really understand who he is by the stories that I have told her about him, but why do we always concentrate on the negative. I've told her millions of stories, both good and bad. But, I am sure she is left with those stories that make him look totally like shit and me like an angel. And lord knows that I have not always been so nice, so understanding and loveable. But, I guess when a muthafucka makes you mad you're not prone to be democratic with the information.

I flip through the Arts and Entertainment section of the nytimes. Savion Glover is on the cover, spinning, tapping, flying through space. Dreadlocks dangling over floor - lights encapsulating the whole scene in blue hue – majesty in movement, turning beauty into beautiful. I stare at the photo and think about what is beautiful in my life.

I notice Sonia walking up the street toward the cafe. Her canary yellow dress is drenched in sunshine and her glasses seem to fight off, beautifully, the hard glare of the sun.

She walks as if she was water, the full moon in action. Movement fluid, revealing understated and exaggerated motion, Sonia is definitely a woman. Mami Wata; specifically Yemaya, in the flesh, bluish-white waves crashing against rocks on the shore of any dream beach. She resembles the perfect fluid mixture of the African water goddess and her Grecian twin sister, Aphrodite. Her breasts are free as they are revealed, although momentarily, from the thin material holding them back from the world. When she sees me her smile is big and beautiful. I think of my tongue on her nipples and laugh.

"What you laughing at boy?" Mother.
"I was thinking of you and me the last time." I say sheepishly, not trying to start no shit with her before I go to LA. That would definitely be a mess.

"You better stop all of that thinking boy, before I have to take you upstairs and give you some more." She lowers the material on her chest to show dark brown flesh circling the left nipple of her perfect breasts. We both laugh as I go inside of the café to order another cappuccino.

"Thanks baby."

"Where were you coming from? It's fairly early for a party girl like you to be up, isn't it?" Moon.

"I could say the same thing for you, but I have not been partying for awhile. I have to be honest Freddie, there is too much sex when I party and sometimes I don't even remember who it is that I just fucked. And that shit is crazy, man." She sips from her cappuccino adding more sugar.

"Anyway, to answer your question I just came from Laura's house. She lives pretty close to me. I slept over there last night."
"Laura?"
"Yeah, this fine ass Spanish girl from Barcelona. She is so amazing - I truly love her, I think. Well, let's not start there. I think she is an amazing woman, and I would love to get to know her better. Since, I have been sober for the last three weeks, I have been able to, like, get to know her and not sexually, you know? Just hang and talk. We've kind of been attached at the hip for the last two weeks. You know how us Lesbians do, one week to be in love and the next week to plan our future."
"Where did you meet her?"

"Um, at an AA meeting." Sonia lowers her head and picks up one of my dunhills and lights it. Her deep pulls from the cigarette are the only sounds coming from either of us. I light a dunhill.

"AA?" I finally respond.

"Yeah, baby, NA too. I need to slow this shit down. I'm just not working when I'm so fucked up Freddie... You know what I mean? It just seems to be this long night that never ends; like some horror movie. I just couldn't do it any longer. I mean, I'm taking it one day at a time, you know."

"Yeah. Like, hi my name is Frederic and I am a co-dependent, sex addicted, cokehead, alcoholic? Hi Fredric!" I laugh out loud, barely noticing Sonia's face tightening.

"You know you could be a little more supportive, asshole. It's not like it is something that is going to hurt me. (a breath) I just feel like if I don't do it now, I'm a goner." Sonia's temperament is sobering, and I realize that I may have hurt her feelings with my jokes. Moody.

"No, girl, I hear you. These last two days are the first days I can remember being sober. So, I feel you definitely; I just did not know what to say when you said what you said."

"It's not like we have not talked about this before."
"But, we've been blasted out of our heads when we talked about being sober. Like some denied reality that we just need to bring to light, but since we were so high, I just never stuck with that idea further than the conception of it. And since I would probably take sixty more lines after that thought, I just buried it under all of the other shit."

"Freddie, that's precisely the point. How long will you bury shit, brother? I mean it is hard enough to deal with what we have to deal with. It becomes even more difficult to deal when we are constantly piling shit on top of older shit. I just don't want to be thirty and shit - all fucked up and out of it for no particular reason. You know, I've been to these meetings with folks kickin' drugs and alcohol, and let me tell you, we are in a good place to stop using. At least we do not have some sort of mental problem because of our drug usage. Man, Freddie, there are some fucked up people out here. Taking time to listen has helped me see how I can get myself back on track." Message.

"Wow. That sounds like a lot. I think, though, I'm not ready to be all chummy with these types. I'm still caught up in my addictions, and I like them. I'm just kidding, I think. Actually, I just had a crazy ass dream with all this reference to me fucked up on hella drugs and living without Bryan and the school stuff and..."

"And all that shit you've been burying deeper inside. Exactly my point bruh, you need to stop burying shit. It sounds like it's coming out of..."

"My dreams Sherlock, this is my story, okay. You can analyze it as much as you want with your 'new twelve step processed - I'm okay attitude', but I'm not trying to hear it. I'm just not."

My phone rings, and it saves, I think, our relationship. At least it saves my ears from listening to Mami Wata or Mother Superior or whatever over here. I did not mean to be so jumpy at her, but I don't want to keep hearing the same line from everyone who quits for a week or two, or even better and more honorable they quit for a whole month. And since I don't quit, I get to hear them proclaim their newfound sense of self and idealism, until it just gets too hard to deal with. I mean everything just gets so difficult and then your standing on a corner waiting for the man to make the drop, seal the deal, close the book on this week in sobriety. I've seen it all before. I've listened to the **never going to do drugs again** and the **never should've done drugs in the first place story** and I'm tired of it.

Their story and my own.

"Hold on girl…..
Hello?" **RESTRICTED** call #2.
"Hey man. It's me. It's Bryan."
"Yo, what's up with you? I'm getting ready to come see you, baby."
"Well, I'm not in Los Angeles any longer. I'm heading to London." Bryan's voice sounds fairly straightforward and honest - I kind of think he is telling the truth, but he has to be joking, right?

"Hold, On Bryan. Sonia, I'm going to have to take this call. Did you want to hang out any longer?"

If I could only prevent my smart-ass attitude to chill at intense moments in my life, but I can't and the words come out of my mouth like daggers aimed at an enemy I mean to hurt.

Flabbergasted, "Um, no. Fred." Sonia's head lowers as her hand reaches for a few cigarettes to take with her. "Okay, Fred. I'm out. Sorry for giving a fuck about you and your health. Don't call me, okay?" Sonia's eyes full of tears, her manic movements are so fast she almost forgets her scarf on the table. Memory.

I watch her as her little body drifts quickly from the café and through the tree-lined city streets. I had no emotion when I returned to Bryan's call. With Sonia gone, he has me now.

"What was that?" Bryan asks.
"Sonia and I are no longer friends, I think. I just had an epiphany. I don't need anyone in my life telling me what I should do, especially her. Anyway, where are you?"
"Well, I'm on my way to London right now. (silence) Don't be mad. I still have all of the plans arranged. A limo will pick you up from LAX, so look for the guy holding the sign with your name. I have the limo fully stocked and am fucking sad too, because I thought we would be able to

have some fun on the ride from the airport to the hotel; which, my friend is nicer than the W in New York. Don't tell your mum I said that. I'll be back in town Monday. I know this is weird, but my company and I just sealed an amazing deal with a company in the UK, and I am off to make sure all of the numbers add up and all the t's are crossed. What's that silly saying?"

"I don't know what that saying is; I know I'm a little sad though." I whisper, looking desperately into the empty coffee mugs on the café table.

"Well, you should not have yelled at her. I'd be sad too, if I just lost my friend."
"What are you talking about? Sonia? I'm not thinking about her, I'm sad because I wanted to see you. I mean we was suppose already be in each other's arms baby."
"Hey, don't get all hot and bothered with me, baby. I'm going to see you in a minute, and then we can get hot and bothered together. I just have to secure this deal. You will be proud of me; I'm getting one hell of a commission on this one. We can buy a house. I know this is so out of left field, but I had been thinking, and saving, and.... (silence) Seriously, I can put it down, and we can get serious, get

married, even. I don't give a fuck; we can do this my ninja."

You know how you know something. I mean really know a thing. It's just what it is, no denial and no pretense. You just know. Like the sun comes up in the morning and goes down at night - and the moon comes out and night goes back again in the morning. Like I know my name, I know when I am getting hot and when I am cold. You just know. I know this mutha fucka loves me, and I love him. He would do anything he could for me, and I want him so much to be in my life. I know I want to be next to him. I know that all of the love that I feel for him is still overshadowed by the love I also feel for William. I know I should just sit in the hotel in LA and relax, eat, rest, read and wait for my Bryan, my man. I know all of this, and I know exactly what I am going to do. I just know.

drink_6

Air conditioning feels so good until you have to step back out into the hot ass desert heat. Then it just feels like temporal satisfaction, an easy fix; like everything else. But, I can't complain. I could be walking or on one of those foreign buses that I see people riding in Los Angeles. The whole time I was in LA I never rode in one of those.

It's always so damn hot in Los Angeles.

Sitting in the back of the limo I can see the heat breathing off of the concrete, as if hell was concealed somewhere below the pavement. Inside this cold ass car the sweater I tucked away in my luggage, just for these situations, was barely enough to keep me warm. I do not think I ever liked AC. I appreciate it, but I don't like it. Without it I think the whole of LA would burn up and disappear into thin air. Burn like the heat rising from the concrete slabs connecting this long, unending, unrelenting city of smoggy-ass dreams and lost angels- wings clipped, littering the freeway shoulder.

When Bryan said the limo would be hooked up he was not kidding. A fully stocked liquor cabinet, five hundred dvds to choose from, any artist whoever made music to listen to, and a small library of my favorite authors, Hesse, Walker, Baldwin, Thoreau and Coelho. I could have driven back and forth from the bay area to LA fifty times and still not consumed all of the delicacies of this limousine. This mutha fucka even had coke in the liquor cabinet. After I made a greyhound, of course, I had to do a few lines, I know it is only six o'clock, but it's going to be a long ride from LAX to the hotel downtown. Traffic is her name, and LA has made her famous.

I call Bryan, but he does not answer. My message is sexy, short and cute.

..hey nigga. Just wanted to let you know that I found your surprise in the liquor cabinet. I'm holding my dick with my hands, waiting till you can do the same, but with your hands of course. I'll be waiting.

I do a few more lines and smile at my reflection in the window separating the driver from me. Sometimes when I do my first line of cocaine I feel a rush of blood to my head, and the calm comes in and takes over me. I lower the window dividing me from the chauffeur and ask how much longer the drive to the hotel is going to be. I barely remember seeing the man when I got off the plane, but now I can see how fine he is.

"The Myokya Hotel is about an hour and a half away with all of this traffic. Would you like to watch a dvd, or listen to some music? You can control everything from back there," He smiles, and I can see how beautiful his headshot must be so I ask,
"You an actor?"
"How did you know? Is it that obvious?"
"No, I just thought you had such a beautiful smile you must be an actor or a model."
"Thanks. You have a great smile too. What do you do for a living?"
"This. I just fly in and out of cities, ride in limos with fine ass chauffeurs and do coke in the back seat. It's a fairly easy life for me, but costly for my financiers."

I laugh out loud and so does he. I notice that he is staring at me pretty intensely in the rear view mirror. Maybe he can take my mind off the fact that deep down inside I am a bit terrified to be back in LA so soon. Maybe, it's the drugs that allow me to avoid all of this fear shit and being afraid. I do know that I won't deal with it at all today and this man's sexy smile is the reason. Tomorrow, William will be here, and then Bryan will end my week. And I won't have to deal with any of it at all. I will continue to be fearless. Or at least, ambivalent.

"Can I have a bump? I'm sorry is that not a cool thing to ask?"
"Since you asked, it's cool. It would not be cool, if you were afraid and did not ask, you know? Anyway, I have so much back here I should share."

I hand him a key with an anthill of coke on the edge. When he grabs the key, he sniffs all of the coke into his left nostril. His hand holds my hand as he attempts to watch the road, do cocaine and drive at the same time. We repeat the same action, his hand holding mine while he sniffs the hill of cocaine into his right nostril this time. The LA traffic stillness provides the needed stationary occasion for such encounters.

"What's your name?" I ask as I make another line for myself. He waits to answer until I look up and meet his eyes in the rear-view mirror.

"Santiago-Amal." He answers with that fucking smile and those damn fucking pretty ass white teeth.
"Well Santiago, my name is Frederic Leon, I know - forgive the French names. My mother was in love with her French teacher, thus - Frederic and Leon."

Reaching out my hand to shake his, he holds on, our handshake lingering into his fingers massaging my hand. Since, the traffic is standstill, I am flattered, and I smile back at him. He holds on to my hand. When I try to release his grip, he does not want to let go so I give in again. When he finally lets go, I notice that he has put his right blinker on to exit the chain-linked fence known as the LA freeways.

"I'm going to try and get off of this free-way and take the streets, it'll be faster." He smiles, almost not even moving his mouth, just teeth and lips, beautiful and frozen in my head as such.

"But, then that means you will be gone. I don't want it to be faster. I want it to linger like our hand shake, sweaty palms and shit like that."

"You know, I'm your driver until Monday, right?" he says again with this smile that if you could see it, you'd agree he is making us both wet.

"Oh… you mean you can't leave my side until Monday?" Sly, smooth, and sardonic, I hear myself and laugh a little.

"Well, only when you want me to wait in the car. Most people leave me in the car until they are ready for me again."

(Thank God for rearview mirrors!)

"What do you mean ready?"

"You know ready for me to drive them where they want to go."

"What if I want you to hang out with me tonight. You know, hang out in the hotel. Maybe change clothes and get a cab and go out on the town?" The way we both smile makes me glad that I asked, and I'm starting to get giddy about our date tonight. Somehow I am always planning a way to not be alone.

We arrive at the Myokya Hotel, Santiago parks the limo in the VIP section of the parking lot. I never really thought about how much money Bryan made until today or really how. I mean, I knew it was commercial-real-estate-something-or-the-other, but it was one of those jobs someone explains, and then you just nod your head as if you understood even though both people realize the explanation didn't make sense.

This hotel is immaculate and fucking expensive. The room, a bi-level penthouse suite with a Jacuzzi, a 360 degree view of the whole fucking state of California it seems, and a mirrored ceiling; and this is where I am sleeping tonight. Flowers invade every inch of the room, bottles of wine, chilled champagne, fruit and cheese plates everywhere. This must be what heaven looks like, I joke to Santiago.

I follow Santiago as he walks to each window. I stand a few feet behind him, still close enough to smell him, see his back through his shirt. He smiles as he moves around the room, inching away as I get closer. I stop and retrace my steps, looking for the bag of cocaine. I make a few lines while Santiago opens the first bottle of wine.

He sits down next to me and hands me my glass of Merlot from some small vineyard in southern Spain. We toast to the moment and the sheer luck of this situation. He does a few lines, and I wait till my first glass is empty before I join him. The room is getting hot, and I take my shirt off. Santiago follows suit to my surprise, and I notice how fit we both are in the mirror above head. I stare intently at his back in the mirror. There is something about looking at someone who you can touch with ease, but you don't yet because now you have become a voyeur, and now it's all about watching, searching for more things to see and not be seen.

Santiago's hand moves from the bottom of my back to my neck. He grabs my neck with a little force, nipples stiffen, d_ick present. Like being set free from caged realities, Santiago takes me in his arms, upstairs to the Jacuzzi. He pushes me on the hardwood bench and catches me as I fall backwards. He begins to take off his clothes. One hand is holding me down, while the other undresses himself. His naked body is brown caramel, similar to Bryan, but this body is sun-drenched brasilian man, ocean stained. These hands huge hammocks holding me, swaying me. I stare at his massive thighs and penis erect and slightly leaning left.

Like trees on the lower level of the rainforest, thick with history, aged beauty. I follow with my lips till they meet him, forcefully entering mouth. Tongue engages its fullness, and I taste salty remnants of sexual preliminaries. I begin to unbutton my pants and his hands reach for my penis, erect. He sticks his fingers into his mouth. Wet fingers begin to move softly back and forth on my penis. My mouth engages his penis further, and I laugh internally, cause this feels so good. He feels so good. He looks so good. It feels so good.

We slowly enter the Jacuzzi, and we both hold each other in the bubbling hot water. Looking into his eyes, I smile and so does he. He holds onto me, and it feels like he is never going to let go. I hold him back just as hard. Standing up in the middle of a somewhere that I have never been, barely breathing, but seeing fully everything becoming more tangible, more real. With a man, I do not know, but feel as though I've known for longer than two and a half hours. He begins to kiss my ears, his hands move from my waist to my ass, clinching. He grabs unto my flesh and holds hard, his tongue has moved from ear to face, to tongue. We kiss passionately and forcefully until I turn away to gasp for air. The heat from the Jacuzzi and his brown hard body takes me under. I feel like I am drowning, and his lungs are my savior, my oxygen tank. His chest is my life preserver that holds me freely in shallow water. Investigating fully each other's body, we move from the Jacuzzi to the master bedroom. Red walls and famous post modern and pop-art prints adorn this room, so many images to take me away and into the possibility of this encounter, this now.

He enters me, and I feel closer to his grandmother. 'Tita mia', I scream, 'abuela.' He begins to mumble portugese into my ear, as his pelvis moves forcefully faster with quick penetration in and out, and out and in, banging against my ass and lower back. Blood and temperatures rise, hands reach to grab hair. Santiago is forceful. Rough and sweet, but he is very strong. At times, I feel closer to fear than passion and that excites me a bit. Frightens me as well. Who is he?

He is moving so fast that I can't catch my breath fast or long enough to keep one thought from melting into another. He slows down his pace enough for me to catch my breath, and meet his pace with my hips. I open my mouth slightly and breathe in his smell. He smells so foreign, a remembering of a past life. Sun kissed papaya and limon, or fresh flowers float through his melanin rich skin. He takes himself out of me and rests on my back. His penis still hard and breathing, both of us together of the same breathe. He grabs my penis and leads it toward his ass. As I enter him, I feel myself falling. Like angels from heaven, I am wingless, but still airborne, still divine. Free, but landing soon. As I pump faster and slower and then faster again, his Portugese ramblings become louder, and I begin to scream with him. "Tita Mia, Abuela!" As if he was my second language and I his translation, he defines me in a language I do not know. We both climax at the same time, and I lie silently in between now and then, forever beckoning. He holds me. I hold unto him. We close our eyes and fall into slumber, logs drifting down the rainforest's river, constantly moving forward, bumping, crashing against rocks, but moving still.

Santiago walks out from the shower with towel in hand, droplets of water cling unto his brown body like oxygen in lungs. He stands in front of me, thinking me sleep. His body glistens in the steamy red light streaming from the open bathroom door. He smiles down at me and lowers his head to kiss me on the cheek. I turn my head meet his lips with mine. We kiss for a long time, and I suck his tongue like a *now-and-later* till all of the sweet sugar is gone and my tongue and his turn a different color from the flavor.

"You're awake, huh?"

We both laugh, and he lies down next to me.

"I should take a shower too... I don't want to get you all dirty."

"Is it alright for me to just lie here while you shower?"

"You can do whatever you want. Just remember that, okay?" Sauntering into the bathroom I begin humming John Coltrane's 'Greensleeves.

The water, hard and cleansing, washes me anew. Like a fresh water stream, I cleanse all of my past and future problems away. When I exit, Santiago is laying on his back staring at himself in the mirror. I dry myself off and lie next to him. For a moment, I think that I could love so many people. Almost one person for every day of the year. My arms have held so many men and so many women. Sometimes it feels that I am left with the remains of the day - their hearts, or pieces of them that have attached to me, or shards of my own heart under my foot. I dance in this

awareness, this sea that my ship sails for freedom, clarity,
something past because I know I'm searching for
something and it must be in the past, right? He hands me
the cd cover with our constructed lines covering the photo
of a city skyline.

"Looks like it is snowing in that city, huh?"

"Yea, like a snowy day in Chicago, right?" I say. "Did you
ever read that book, A Snowy Day, by Ezra Jack Keats?

"No." Santiago replies snorting a line from the winter's
snow fall.

drink_7

In the morning, like 6 a.m., my phone rings:
RESTRICTED. William.
"Hey, who you wit'? (pause) I'm just playing. Hey Baby!"
His voice sounds alert and awake, the complete opposite of
mine; rough edges, sordid experiences, sharp tones and
blood shot eyes.

"I'm laid out. You must be magical, cause I don't know
how I even heard this call. I am happy that I did though.
How are you?"

"Where you at? I thought you '*was*' coming here
yesterday? I got so much to talk to you about." His voice
excited and anxious.

I begin to answer and a large body restricts my movement.
Who the fuck is on me? I open my eyes and remember him
well. Oh shit.

"William, man, it's hecka early, right now. You want to
meet for breakfast in a bit?" Hurrying off the phone.

"Hecka?" William laughs and clears his throat. "That sounds good. You want me to come get you? Where you at?"

"Uh, the Myakyo Hotel downtown LA. Come get me."

"Cool, I'll call at the normal people time. Sorry for calling so early. I'm just excited to see you. I got a full day planned for us. You're gonna flip."

This sounds good. This man feels good. I actually am feeling good despite the time, the weight on my rib cage, and my usual headache.

"Alright… hit me up then."

We both hang up, and I lie under Santiago knowing that soon I will have to leave. He feels good; something about his warmth is comforting to me. It makes me feel safe. I think about touching his ass then my hand moves there. He moves slightly, still asleep. I think of my tongue on his neck and then it is there, wet flesh. He moves more, penis slightly erect, tongue now to ear. We engage the moment, or morning blessing for men. Well, I don't know about all men, but when I wake up my dick is as hard as a baseball bat in the world series.

When we finish Santiago falls back to sleep instantly. As if the moment he came, his body sent a signal that told him it was time to go back to sleep, and he obediently followed. I begin moving from under Santiago's body weight, he a brick wall, all dense flesh, brown muscles and every bit a man. I guess I didn't notice how big he was. I jaunt to the shower and realize exactly what happened yesterday. I smile, and I'm glad William called me. I might have stayed in this relationship, in this room, with this man, the whole weekend.

"Oh, I guess the dream is over. I figured it was a lot to ask, to actually receive and I would like to thank you for your time brother. (yawn) I think you are cool Frederic. You know, a great guy. I hope we can still be friends (yawn)?" Santiago's eyes: so sincere. Santiago's words: touch my heart.

"Hey man, I'm still going to be around. You know, we can still be close. I'll need my driver and shit. I'm just going to breakfast."

"Okay, boss." Santiago searches for his clothes as the bathroom door closes.

The shower hot and cleansing, I let the steam fill my nostrils and emotions. I concentrate my thoughts only on myself; and William, of course. What on earth could this guy think we were doing? Duh, just fucking. That's all I was in it for. I mean just because I have to go doesn't mean we won't see each other again. I mean there is the ride back to the airport. That's the only thing about a one-night stand or fucking someone on the first date. Sometimes they want to come back. It's like a title to a horror movie.

By the time I dry off and walk out of the shower, the entire suite has been cleaned and re-stocked. Santiago is nowhere to be found. I light a cigarette and walk to the window. Pressing my naked body against the glass, inhaling smoke. I love when my naked body is up against glass, love the feeling it gives me. I imagine William's body and his lips against mine. He was the best kisser I have ever been with. Not only because he could kiss, but he had this philosophy about kissing that restricted us from linking lips for quite awhile. It made him mysterious and me intrigued, annoyed, but intrigued mostly.

"Well, see I don't kiss just anyone. Not that you are just anyone Frederic, but I'm not there right now. I mean…. We have a long time together, and I want to know that when I kiss you I am with you. Not just my feelings for you but all of you and all of me, a real kiss. Our mouths. Together. Where breath lives, we breathe together without intention, without purpose? Not me. I want to find purpose inside of you, friend. I want to mean to kiss you."

This was a long time ago mind you, but I still get a little bit unnerved when I think about. His words were so confusing, but honorable? I could not figure out my feelings. I knew he loved me, and I loved him. But, he held out for like three months before he would even kiss me. I mean he would kiss me on the lips, but not "kiss" me for what seemed to be forever. At the time, I just followed his lead. I kind of already knew that I would be with this man for a long time. And to keep it slow was not so bad, right?

As the glass and I make love over the downtown Los Angeles morning, I reminisce about a love that is so close and yet so far away through the hazy, dense morning fog. Transparent shards of glass, beautiful and dangerously cutting, sharp edges, spiraling reflections.

Coming from to go toward, returning to meet him again in Los Angeles, of all places. I was totally dreading coming to Los Angeles, not because of William, but because Los Angeles was the place where I lost everything and kind of sort of found myself. I guess, I was afraid to return because of William, but knew something in my return was kind of funny. The humor is what is pulling me toward him. "Them that's got shall have."

I want to have me. I break free from previous assumptions of the weight of the love that I have for this man, and I am again anxious. Like a first date, I feel a bit nervous and shy. The window and I exchange pleasantries, and I walk back into the bathroom to get prepared for my date. I want to see my time with William as a date. A time to see each other again; for the first time possibly. I want to see what parts of me are in love with him. What parts get excited when he saunters in and dances for the camera, smiles, and sings for me?

9:45 a.m.

Phone rings. I answer. William is downstairs. Grab wallet. Shoes on. Hat, key- door lock. Elevator. L= Lobby.

Santiago. "No, car today. See you later." Smile, wink. Black Lexus hard top, 2 door.. Door open. Lips. William. Door shut. Lips. William. Hand. Thighs. Lips. William. Tongues. William. Hands. Horn…blowing. Wiliam. Hands. On. Thigh. Wiliam. Lips. Horns. People Yelling. Time. Passes. William. Lips.

"I'm gonna start driving now." William pulls his lips away, grabs keys, car moves. Staring hungrily, locked eyes and all, I sit back in seat, finger in mouth, still breathing, in and out, frequent repetitions. I'm still alive I think to myself.

William drives through the LA traffic like a pro, I imagined this type of reception when I first arrived, two years or so ago. I mean could you imagine the growth we would have had in that time till now?

Do you think like that sometimes? The "what ifs?" I try not to but sometimes I think what would have happened if I would have had what I wanted? You know, the thing you want actually going right? Like William greeting me when I first arrived and him and I living together here in LA together. Just to think of that makes me so sad. I'm sitting here with the man who made me the saddest I have ever felt in my life. I just fucking made out with this same man. I'm such a Frederic.

We drive in silence, and I do not ask where we are going. I don't care. I want to not care. I want to fall again in this man's world and have my space there and live again. I think about who I am and whom I have become, and I realize that a lot of what makes me, me, is William.

Staring out the car window reminds me of trips on the greyhound, driving endless miles through our subconscious, illuminated, manifested in the horizons' design. William is like these roads, long and slick, five lanes at a time, 70 mph speed limits; a beautiful dream full of images within themselves. Falling again and I am awaiting the ground, the falls' actualization. The moment in which falling becomes totally real - when you land on your face.

Today, as my hand rests on William's thigh, my mind encapsulated in what it must feel like for William to have my hand there, and my feelings that we would meet again proven true like I hoped. I hear jazz when I am this happy and especially when I am with William. And some say it seems like it was yesterday, a jazz club enclosing this possibility is where we met. Introduced by a dear friend, but our eyes met way before.

@1999

"Welcome to the Velvet Lounge. I am your host tonight, Sojourn. You are in for a treat, tonight we present the first installment of *speak easy,* a monthly poetry, dance and jazz-fusion. First to the stage I would like to bring up Frederic, Jonavive and Blaq presenting for you tonight their group piece entitled, *wonderful, beautiful, divine.*"

The club, a small closet with a huge stage, square tables, plaid wall paper, black owned, jazz great with little money and big talent. Saucy waitress named Devine with big hair, big attitude, and honestly just an overall big woman. Records taped on the wall, mostly uneven. Cool twenty-somethings litter the space, University of Chicago students and artists mainly. They wear bright colors, sweaters thick, most with scarves hand-made all possessing a hip flavor for days. Protected from the icy cold of the city in November. Chicago is white steel cold in the winter.

Mouth open. Microphone captures words, I bust.

this system, full of denial - petty circumstances for war
ruining favor from the divine with sublime military invasion
outside
influencing nations with ill-articulated banter, spinning
information so out of control that your children fall
through the holes, but since they are your children, they are
white
they are caught by fathers' law degree
mother's ill regard and sympathy
children more fucked up than me but the hatred that you
perpetuate has eliminated cultures, soldiers have died for
your gold....

As I open my eyes, words still fierce and moving forward, I
caught his eye and believe that was the moment that I knew
I would love him forever. He was wearing an orange and
brown plaid paint-boy cap, a grey sweater and dark brown
khakis. From the stage, I sent him myself. He rose and
walked toward the restroom entrance, in the midst of my
poem my eyes directed toward his, smiling.

this aint my nor your system
let's pull together and articulate wisdom
and
shine baby shine
like the great divine….

I exited the stage as if it was choreographed. People clapped, Blaq began dancing and Jonivive played her ethereal flute. As my last foot left the stage and landed on the floor, Lona interrupted me walking toward William, (then he was just my heart, without the name, a face without a history – only this moment now mattered.)

"Hey boy, that was great." Lona hugged me hard and whispered in my ear, "I want you to meet my boy. He's standing right behind me." She points to him, I smile, we meet, he says his name, I say mine, we stare, his eyes, my mouth and his, we both smile, we talk for a minute, he sits back down, I get back on stage, as if it was planned and finish the set.

"What you thinking about right now?" Out of nowhere words dance through my thoughts of our first meeting.

Before I can respond I feel the wind hit my face and see the mountains firm and picturesque in the distance.

"Honestly, I was remembering when Lona introduced us."
"You mean when you ran off the stage while you were performing to meet me at the restroom?" William's voice like childhood friend, brother on playground holding hands in the sand box, laughing, together forever again.

"Yea exactly baby. Can I ask what you was thinking about?"
"Well, since you were honest, I was thinking about you and how you were doing with the way we left it - and all the bull shit I know I put you through. I mean you had just got arrested in your school, came out to Los Angeles for some comfort and safety, to me, and I just disappeared. I've been thinking about that for awhile."

As if I was writing this book, had some influence in what you were reading, William spoke everything I've been waiting to hear for years it seems. I mean, he is not even finished talking right now, I just interrupted this part of the book to say, *damn, this is what I want to hear*.

"......I just feel like I could and should have given you better. You deserve better Frederic. Me leaving was wrapped up in so much of the bullshit that I was dealing with at the time. If I may, I would like to say that I was a different person back then, just not able to differentiate between what was real and what was not. LA can do that to you sometimes. It just embeds you in its façade for the sheer fact that all of the work that we do is illusionary or make believe. We make you feel something or buy something because of what we do or what we look like. And all the while I don't feel a damn thing. I just want to get paid. The whole industry is like that I think. No excuse, I know I am an asshole."

The ride continues, as if this episode did not even happen, in silence. I smile, my hand remains on Williams' thigh the entire time, and I feel good. I feel like we are driving back to the bay area, but of course we aren't. I am enjoying having no control over the situation right now, and I also feel inspired to do something because of what I just heard. You know the first time I've felt creative in a minute, and it really has everything to do with Williams' presence this time.

Each passing bit of nature caresses my eyes, illuminates my spirits and raises the stakes and my hopes for something or someone tangible that I can hold unto. Something beautiful to say I am. Reflection eternal. External reasons to look within and analyze the beautiful bit of nature inside. I am open, as these skies and my mind. William holds me in this space, this car, leather seats, fallen fear and determined bliss. I remember what it feels like to love someone, not just like. Not just to be with someone but to know someone and want to continue on the journey of knowing. Not just sleeping with someone but connecting souls, a communal puzzle of copulation and intellectual reunion. Like when you meditate, centering on your center, concentrating on your breath and being with the eternal. And then the tears, when you are open and the eternal spirit runs through you like a river meandering and winding toward the mouth of heaven. He becomes the space in between when we unite. I am reminded of my behavior, faults, and successes. Reminded of how far I have fallen since William left, how my own heart has not been allowed to even beat as melodic and sincere as it use to. How I gave up when William left. I remember the fights and the arguments my jealously caused, and I ease up. There is enough fault between the

both of us to go around as to why we are not together. The
real question is where are we going with this now?

William pulls the car off the freeway and drives down and
through a forest.

"Um, I hate to ruin the surprise, but where are we going?" I
ask timidly.
"I'm not telling. Just a little bit longer man, you ain't got no
where to go do you?" And just like that the smile that
lingers, lasts and even scars cheekbones in its hopeful
permanence was tattooed on my face forever. I don't say
anything, he smiles back, we continue forward, I laugh out
loud, he reminds me of when he met my mother, I remind
him of me meeting his, we kiss briefly, and he parks near a
huge sign reading *Welcome To The Coeloah Hot Springs.*

All I can do is smile. I always wanted to go to a hot spring
area in California. Everyone I knew in the bay area spoke
lavishly about the accessibility of the hot springs and how
great the water was for the spirit. The sun was shining as I
exited the car. Green surrounded us as we enter calmly our
newest fairy tale. We walked through the trees as the wind

blew and cooled us at times. When my body is hot, my whole body gets hot. All I wanted to do was cool off.

The area reminded me of some of the Cenotes we went to when we were in Tulum, Mexico, on the Yucatan Riviera. Cenotes are natural water sources, sometimes underneath caves, and hidden deep in the jungles, or forests.

That was our first trip together, William and I. We stayed at this chic hotel/café/restaurant named Luna Maya. The owner was from the Spain, and we immediately fell in love with the orange, light blue, white and brown color palette used to decorate the space. It felt like we could have been in any city in the world, but the hotel also simultaneously felt distinctly Mexican. I remember being happy then. William and I walked hand and hand into the reception area. I remembered when we couldn't do that. Well, I couldn't. I was afraid. Of what, I don't actually know. I knew everyone had suspicions that I was queer or something. But since suspicions allege some sort of wrong-doing I did not want to prove them right in their assessment. I didn't want to be in no parades, walk through no gay clubs so I ran fiercely from the word queer and any identity-related-anything. Which led to the first time we broke up.

"You know, you can fuck me and be all up in my shit with your jealous ass and your crazy ass tendencies, but you can't hold my muthafucking hand in public, like I'm some kind of virus or something.

Or maybe, you are the virus and you want to protect me by not holding my hand and having everyone think I am the fucking sick one. What the fuck is it Frederic? Tell me?" There were no words. He was right. We had so many issues. But I think the attraction and the commonality of experiences kept us close to each other, as if we've both been made co-dependent by this ordeal of being both homosexual and black, and in love with each other. Being a black boy is hard enough. And to begin to claim being homosexual on top of that is quite a brave decision. I can't say that I was too excited to go out screaming that I was in love with another black man. That I loved how we fit together when we were naked, how the light bounced off of our negro skin. The most hated, both finding the most love they have ever felt in their lives by loving each other.

He makes me feel complete and safe. Human even. For some reason when you want to be with your equal it is that much harder to make it work. Like the challenge is actually seeing yourself with anyone, and then when all the shit you've created to block your heart starts to fall, we get all protective of the walls falling and run to pick up more bricks and cement to build those walls up again. So much to deal with loving another person, especially when you're black and male and you love black males. And since this man is real, and I am real and we are together, I am actually feeling transformed for the road I've traveled. Feeling like my hands touching this back with all of the years between us actually means something, not just a random back, but a back belonging to my lover, not random at all.

William and I walk into the room, and he shuts the door behind us. The room number is 1113. I laugh because I know he asked if they had this room number. This was the number of the room where we first went to hook up officially. We couldn't do it at either one of our places because of our roommates. They both would have tripped out. I hate when people don't actually recognize what they see and accept it. Everyone I knew had a question of my sexuality, but no one would ask me anything. Literally, I would have people asking me when I was getting married. They knew they never saw me with a woman; the only person they ever saw me with was William.

Autumn again, harvesting in him, his arms, my arms, my hands sculpting his back, full of him in my arms, his head resting on my neck, me panting and breathing harder, just cause. 'I just want to hold you' I say to him and we do, for what seems an eternity. My arms enclose him like the wind weathering heights, atop of mountains, snowcapped fire.

It is almost eleven in the evening when I wake up.

I am naked again and press my body against the window, the cold glass. Trees as far as my eyes can see and more trees behind these, and these trees resemble seedlings from family trees. Huge trunks of trees resemble these huge pillars of childhood forests ran through. Lost in them, I see myself searching for my father. Walking through these trees, running at times, still searching for my feeble beginnings, cutting myself from the outstretched branches and my quick movements. Running through a forest of abuse, from idle hands and stares and glances from family members, trees, elders who misinterpret my beauty, always

reaching and grabbing, trying to capture the innocence.
Not to be touched, you can't touch me, or at least hold me
down too long, I ran and fell and got back up and ran
again. I ran from these arms of aging bark and idle
branches, wisdom defunct. I ran into me. My eyes reflected
back tears and truths unable to digest prior, but open in
this space, these trees, my eyes have seen before. Was this
what I've been running from? What I've been running for?
A pain attacks my head as the trees begin to blur.

"Frederic?" His words loud shock me. Pulled back from my
daze, quick movement, feet slip on towel below, body's
weight breaking window, reaching for something to grab,
hearing my body break through glass, shards of glass, too
fast, I move, twist, fall, red, breaking glass, window, blood
runs deeper than river's edge. My body lands hard on the
outside deck. Total blackness.

This glass, shards embedded in skin, my skin,
consciousness comes back like a shooting star, brief, blood
ripping from within, I am bleeding, shouts are heard, it is
William, he is crying, I am falling from grace or something

like that. My hands reach out for him, and I touch his chest, blood drenched. His eyes, steadfast, holding unto me for forever he says, feel numb to my grasp. Eyes flittering back and forth in and out. I can't see William. He is fading, or is it me?

drink # 8_WILLIAM

In my life I've done great things. I always knew I would.
That was the way my family raised me. Ever since I was a
little boy, they, my parents, pushed me to be excellent.
Dance classes ever since I knew how to walk, the best
schools, and a plan that we never strayed from. They taught
by example. Each of them very successful in their own
careers and professions, teaching us children that the only
way to get what you want is to get it yourself. Each of them
carrying forth their family's tradition of doing everything
excellently, never looking back ever, and never letting
anyone get in the way.

Being a first generation Jamaican American had its
advantages. My family came from St. Anne's Parish in
Jamaica and raised me to have "nuff" respect for being
West Indian. I never thought I was less than anyone, no
matter what color they were. I was the best at everything I
did, and I still am.

I remember one time at private school there was this white
boy named Charles who had it in for me. He was the 2nd
ranked student at our school, and I was the 1st. He told our

Head master that I had cheated off of his test. We both got top honors on this test, but I had always had the top mark in this class, while Charles made one error at the beginning of the semester making him two points behind me in cumulative scores. Our teacher said the only way to prove that I didn't cheat was for the both of us to go head to head in an oral test. Since I memorized everything, I was excited to embarrass Charles in front of the whole school. The examination only lasted an hour, and Charles lost because it turned out he had cheated off of me. He was unable to answer most of the questions the teacher asked because he didn't actually read the material. He had studied the answers from the last test, but the teacher gave us different questions from the selected course work. I always felt like this for me was my way at getting back at United States white people, head to head combat, intelligence to intelligence.

Most of the time I challenged myself harder than my parents ever could. For some reason I was never satisfied, and I hope that I never will be. It seems like a waste of time to do something and not do it well. Why the fuck do it? Maybe that's why I left Frederic. Maybe that's why I feel so bad. Maybe, that's what made me take the gig the same day I knew he was coming. I just couldn't believe he had fallen so low. I know it must have been hard for him to lose everything after being arrested at that school, but I couldn't understand why he ran away from the fight.

He was in a space where he continued to doubt himself. I couldn't understand why he decided not to sue those fucking racist cops and instead accept the deal they gave him. He had the media behind him and the whole damn country it seemed. Being a black man who was arrested at the school where he worked, and having that damn videotape as evidence, I just knew he would have taken the bank in a lawsuit. But Frederic was scared. I had never seen him that fearful. Never seen anyone that afraid. We would go out when I came out to San Francisco to be with him, and he would jump every time he saw a police car. Anytime we heard a siren he would look behind his back, as if the car was coming for him.

After awhile I figured he would get over it, but he never did. Talking to the Psychiatrist and going to the PTSD meetings seemed to make everything worse. I guess that is why I invited him to be with me. Maybe that would help him. I know I fucked up; he came to be with me for some sense of salvation, some sense of love. But, I just couldn't see myself losing my life for anyone. We had our problems but that was when he was normal. There was no way I was going to be able to fight with someone who was afraid to fight their own battles. No way I was going to watch as he fell apart and crawled into a ball of human in a corner of my house.

That's where I was wrong. Something in him died, and I felt the killing of Frederic happened inside of my heart. Like him going through all of this took away the man that I loved so much. The man I thought I could be with forever. My Frederic was dead. At least the spirit inside of him was gone. The man I could look into his eyes and know everything was no longer there. There were no problems in Frederic's eyes. The man who I almost lost my parent's love for, was gone. How could I want to be with someone who didn't want to be with them selves anymore? Someone who had lost his own fight? I couldn't imagine losing anymore of him, and I knew that I was not willing to risk all that I had gained for anyone, not even Frederic.

We had a love affair written in the stars.

The moment I saw him on that stage in Chicago that night, I knew he was going to be my man. I knew we were going to be together. Sometimes you just know things, without knowing why you know them. A seed was planted a long time ago, somewhere in a magical space, and he and I were going to grow into this love together. Now, he was sick. He was different, somehow too fragile. Broken to a place where he might never return. For the first time in my life I was afraid. Here was the man who I loved enough to go through hell and back to be with. We had some of the hardest fights I have ever experienced in my life. Our relationship was never easy and that was what made me want to be with him even more. The push and pull. Our love was the energetic experience of life, love, and the pursuit of happiness. He was my new nation, and we were forming it together under the same precepts of this great country. Liberty, freedom, and justice. Now, he was just a victim. Not him at all. Not the man I knew and loved. And not the man I wanted to be with.

All of these trees look the same. Frederic's voice pierces me as I try and lift him from the wreckage. 'What happened?' I hear myself scream. When I said his name he must have slipped and fell, hitting the glass hard, falling, crashing, and now all of this blood. Blood from his limp body, from my feet, my heart. His body is heavy; glass pierces my skin from the shards lodged in his - blood staining my hands. blood staining.

The ambulance shouts loud sneering yelps, and I cannot stand still for much longer, a child is screaming. They, medics, take my Frederic away. I can't ride in the ambulance, not relation, they say. The radio in the car screams loud signals that the world is over, and I believe these words this time. The blood on my shirt speaks of these words; these truths permeate and dry upon my face, crack, and flake red on shirt, red dirt, on hands, and face. I can't decipher whose blood is whose. If Fred does not make it, I'm killing myself tonight. I am ready to die. I refuse to live again without Frederic.

William's BMW drives through the same trees that once welcomed him, now baring its bare branches and swirling dry leaves, as he speeds behind the ambulance carrying his beloved. Summer turned into winter, or autumn after one night of the new equinox, immediately changing. He drives with the weight of guilt enough for three human beings, his own, his father's, and Frederic's. His head a mast, heavy and cold, old - embossed with centuries of pain and past agonies. Finally, again he is alone. He always dreamt of this moment, both nightmarish and blissful, to be alone. But not like this, he thinks to himself.

Just William and no one else.

But his senses alarm his body, and he realizes that this was not what he wanted. He reached out to Frederic because he did not want to be alone anymore. He wanted to be with the only love he ever felt, and now he began to think that he shouldn't have made the whole encounter actually take place. What would he say to Frederic's mother, he thought. Instead of dialing Frederic's mother's number, he quickly dialed Sonia's instead.

"Hello…Sonia?" William's voice was shaking.
"Yes?"
"This is William, I don't know if you remember me, but…."
"Well, I don't speak with your boy anymore so I can't help you find your lost friend." Sonia's voice trails off.

"No, I'm calling because Frederic has been in an accident."
My voice, now not my own, foreign and uneasy.

The silence catches William's attention, he hears sobs.
Sonia holds the phone near her chest and begins to shed the
guarded self she had created since Frederic and she last saw
each other two days ago. It was obvious that Sonia always
loved Frederic and never found it in her heart to hate him,
even though he was so rude and bitchy to her. She knew
that this accident must be drug-related. Her thoughts
rummaged through to the last words they shared that
beautifully sunny, mischievous bright morning. She could
not believe he could be that cruel, but remembered how the
drug used to hold her and make her believe that everyone
else was wrong, not her, never her.

"Um…I'm so sorry William. What drugs are involved in
this one?"

"I don't know what you're talking about? Frederic don't do
drugs, does he?"

"You mean you're not calling to tell me Freddie OD'd or
something?" Sonia sounded confused and a bit irritated.

"No, Fred fell through the glass window in the cabin we
had. I don't know exactly how that happened, 'cause I was

sleeping, but I woke up and called out to Frederic and heard a loud crashing sound. I found Fredric naked, his body, on the ground."

"Oh my god, how is he?" Her voice now sincere and very present.

"I mean… he's pretty bad." William begins to cry out of control and the words that he is speaking are barely audible.

"He can't die Sonia. I know I fucked up, but he just can't die. I'm driving in my car following the ambulance right now."

"Where are you?"

"In Calistoga, I don't know what to do Sonia."

"I thought Freddie was in Los Angeles? What drug are you on William?" Her voice now assured that drugs were involved.

"What's it with you and these drugs, are you okay? We haven't done any drug since we've been together. I don't even do drugs. We took a drive from LA here to go to the hot springs. Damn, it's only been like twelve hours, and he is in the hospital already. I'm kind of fucked up over here. Like, losing-my-mind-fucked-up." William's car swerves left and right behind the ambulance.

"William, tell me where you are, and I will get there immediately. Let me get a pen."

The windowpane is painted white. Probably painted when they bought the old house. Probably painted white for hope. White because of the illusion of perfection, the promise of purity. But the years have turned the beautiful pure white color into a brownish-white, exposed wood, brown screaming from underneath. Worn and weathered, tattered wood creaming through. The constant repetitive action of opening and closing the window, shutting and locking it, either to get some air or protect ourselves from it. And all of this activity leading to its wear, its aging. Peering out of eagerly waiting for something: either coming or going, returning or arriving, staring out of the window waiting. Leaving, at times, all of our emotions for something more, right there on the windowsill. The partition between the here and there, a space in between the now and then.

The doctors say that Frederic is in a coma.
They say he is in critical condition.

They said that some shards of glass were lodged pretty
deep into tissues and extremely close to really important
veins and arteries.

The doctors also said that Frederic had a lot of drugs in his
system.

Cocaine was the drug that they found.

Now, I know what Sonia was talking about.

I also know about Bryan, Frederic's boyfriend.

Sonia says he just arrived in LA to meet Frederic and is on
his way.

Sonia is on her way as well.

She said she would wait for him to get to San Francisco,
and they would drive here together.

I am thinking about leaving.

I can't forgive myself for calling Frederic again.

I can't leave him.

I am not leaving here without him.

----

4 hours later_

William sits in the waiting room of Calistoga General
Hospital, a sprawling well lit, feng-shui'd area with
European fashion magazines, free coffee and espresso, a
playroom and dvd's to watch while you wait. Everything is
so beautiful you forget for a moment that you are here

hoping a love does not die. Since it's off-season in Calistoga, the entire emergency room is empty besides William and the assistant on duty. William's head hangs low as he thinks about the crashing sound that woke him from a beautiful sleep. It sounded like the sky falling down, chicken-little screaming silently, "the sky is falling, the sky is falling."

William tries to fall sleep a few times, but everything he does he hears these words playing in repetition, "the sky is falling, the sky is falling."

William designed something different for this trip; he envisioned him and his man together and forever in union. He actually thought he must have felt a little bit like Frederic did when he moved to Los Angeles. Eager and excited about the pending possibilities of actually making the relationship work, William had very different plans for Calistoga. This time he thought he and Fredric had a chance. Another one. He had just prayed for a long time after he and Frederic had reintroduced themselves to each other physically in the hotel. He had always loved being with Frederic sexually because Fred's aggressive behavior rivaled his and their history made the familiarity of each other's body as necessary and refreshing as water, or war.

Love only felt like this.

He had known this truth once he and Frederic broke up the last time. The final time he had figured. Since then, he had tried to find love with idle passengers, anyone who caught his eye from time to time and still, throughout the adventure, although fun, he found no one who he could trust as much as he trusted Frederic. No one who could hold him the same way Frederic use to. No one he could fight with like Frederic. When Frederic held William it was as if he would be protected forever, safe with no reasons to have to be excellent. He had felt like he was good not because he was smart, or because of his talent, but because God had loved him enough to give him someone like Fredric. The feeling made him cringe even more, as he sat in the hospital waiting room, waiting for an answer, waiting for god.

He had forgiven himself for leaving Frederic and had hoped that Frederic would too. He figured since Frederic had agreed to meet him he must have found a place in his heart to let William back in. At least Frederic had agreed to meet him. William had hoped that the time apart would have helped Frederic come back to himself, even though it was not the best of situations he knew Frederic was strong enough to put the pieces back together again. At least that is what he had hoped. Now he knew that Frederic had been using drugs to put himself back together. He wondered how long this had been going on. Did leaving Frederic lead him into the arms of these new numbing experiences? He would never forgive himself for leaving Frederic if he died.

A woman's voice, loud and shaking breaks William's thoughts. Wiliam looked up to see a beautiful white woman in a cream colored two-piece suit. Her blue scarf dangling, dancing hysterically off her neck as each shaking word from her mouth made her body shake.

"Is Frederic Leon here?" her voice trembling. A man wearing a tweed blazer runs in after Sonia grabbing her hand. William felt another pain in this stomach, this time he had no idea what made him feel this way. He stared intently at the couple, worrying about Frederic, but figuring that the pain in his stomach must be because the man behind her is Frederic's current lover, Bryan.

William had only met Sonia once and it was in the middle of a fight between him and Frederic. Since he did not remember the fight, it must not have been too important, he thought. But he was sure Sonia remembered. Knew in his heart the disdain she must have for him. Especially after he had vanished from Frederic during a time when he should have been there for him. A time that he still can't forgive himself for being so selfish. At least he was there now he thinks to himself, however after the fact.

The couple walked away from the assistant towards William. Sonia and William hugged and began to cry in each other's arms. Bryan's sullen expression caught himself off guard, and William tried to fix his face before he emerged from Sonia's embrace. Arms seemingly so long on such a small girl.

The whole scene kind of freaked Bryan out a bit; he knew Frederic had slept with the entire cast of mourners in the waiting room. He also was a bit pissed off that William and Frederic had hooked up anyway.

Bryan could not understand how the whole thing happened in the first place. He had only found out that he was not going to be in LA the same day he told Frederic. Bryan's head started spinning. Fredrick had abandoned him, even after Bryan had rescued Fredrick from the train stop. Did Frederic call William or did William call Frederic? He wondered if the two had been speaking the whole time he and Frederic had been together. What other lies did Frederic hide in his brain? How crazy, he thought to himself. If all of this happened by coincidence he thought that the world truly was a crazy-ass place. And if so, he sure didn't know if he wanted to know anything else.

William slowly turned to face Bryan. The two men looked a bit shocked, but grabbed the other's extended hand. William pulled Bryan towards him, and the two men hugged. William's tears were the only reason Bryan allowed William to pull him so close. He began to cry as well. They held on to each for some time. Sonia thought it was quite endearing to see these two men hugging in spite of the situation. They all sat down in the waiting room and tried to keep their attention on the subject at hand, Frederic. Bryan's eyes began to wander around the waiting room, avoiding eye contact from both William and Sonia. His head began spinning and he closed his eyes.

Bryan's voice yelled so loud that the assistant dropped the coffee mug he was holding. The loud sound of cracking porcelain hitting the ground added to the shock of Bryan's yell. Sonia and William both turned quickly facing Bryan, eyes, and mouths wide open in surprise. The tears on Bryan's face against the blaring white light of the waiting room haunted William, as he still heard the pain in Bryan's scream ringing long after the cry.

"Bryan, man. Hey, are you alright brother?" William's voice sincere and anxious.

"Not really. Ugh! I'm confused. How did all of this happen? Last time I checked he and you were through. Or better yet, you left him when he moved out to Los Angeles to get away from all the bullshit racist cops and school district shit. I mean, now you two are fucking in a Calistoga hot spring?" Bryan's voice choking and reflective straining from revealing the tears falling quickly from his sullen eyes.

"Um. Bryan, I don't think this is the time or place for all of that." Sonia pulled out a cigarette and walked out of the automatic doors. William's face a blank canvas. William started to rise up and follow Sonia; not having smoked for a few years, this was the perfect time to start again he thought. When William felt Bryan's hand on his arm his body fell back into his seat, and he turned to face Bryan.

William and Bryan stared at each other for a while and then looked off in the distance. Bryan could not believe that he had the nerve to say those things to William out loud. But, at the same time figured this was the only time he would ever have to say these things. This might be the end of all things with Frederic. His heart was heavy for a myriad of reasons and each question felt like a haunting, an accusation and a denial of his own trust in his relationship with Frederic. He figured William's silence was his only answer. How could he say anything? What would he say? William's body rose from his seat as if it was by an outside force. He walked slowly out the revolving door to Sonia. She quietly extended a cigarette and a lighter to him. Tears poured from his eyes as he lit the Dunhill, staring into an empty and unfortunately desolate sky.

drink # 9_SONIA

You all met me at the beginning of this book, chapter one, oops, I mean drink #1, fucking Frederic, always so smart, right. Since he is an alcoholic, his book has to be in drinks, not chapters. So you know just how important that drink, or bump or pill is to Frederic.

Anyway to tell you the straight up truth, I have always loved his smart, big-black-dick-having, always fucking somebody else's life up, ass. He is quite the renaissance man when I come to think of it. The only problem is that he is so self-consumed, always in his head, always engulfed with his own self, and his particular narcissistic way of dealing with things.

Frederic would rather do some drugs when he has a problem then to actually deal with it. Like, the more he would party, the better everything was for him, at least in his head. He was the party animal. Every time I saw him out, he lit up the room like a firefly or a match without end. It seemed like he had energy for all of us. When Frederic hit the dance floor, walked into a room, called you on the phone, emailed you, whatever, it was like your world brightened up a bit. Everything seemed a little bit brighter, better.

I got to say this is bullshit.

I mean this mutha-fucka Frederic is the master of drama, a class act nut job. I hope his ass don't die so I can kill him. I'm serious. This is the most dramatic shit I have ever seen him do.

Bring every one of us to this fucking hospital in the woods, so we can wait to see if he is gonna survive or die. I mean he got us all here, just sitting back without a clue as to what the fuck! Of course I'm concerned and worried about him, but for some reason I guess this is his lesson, his life. I know he is going to survive - he just wanted to see who really loved him, who would be here in his "final" hour. But, what I don't get is what I'm supposed to learn from all of this. I feel like I'm his mother, but I ain't his....

His Mother.

Should I call his mother? I know I'm tripping. I better call his mother. I would want my friends to call my mother if my life was in peril. But what do I say? What do I say to a mother about her son being in a coma, and having fallen through a window? Thank the fuck I'm sober cause this shit could cause someone to do a line of coke, have a drink, or something. 'Shut up Sonia. You know better. We ain't going back down that road.' But, you know what I mean. What would I say to her if I was fucked up?

Shit, I'm sober, and I don't even know what to say.

Sonia had found herself lying face first in an anonymous driveway the day she realized she needed to stop doing drugs. Her bra missing and her panties down past her knees, she had no idea how she had gotten there. She must have blacked out. This was not unlike most of Sonia's sordid nights, except this night she had lost something she would not know how to begin to find. She had to find it, figure it out. If she only knew where she was, she thought to herself.

Sonia stood up, pulling herself together, at least on the surface; luckily she still had her purse wrapped around one shoulder. She pulled out her cell phone, smiling to herself that it was still there too, and called a cab. She sluggishly walked to the corner to see what street she was on. Her whole body ached, and the tears rushed from her eyes like a flash shower, unexpected in its occurrence and its force, but necessary.

She had been raped, she had figured. But maybe not. Sonia couldn't decide which idea to embrace. Her memory began rushing back to her, like her tears, and she pieced enough of the beginning of the night to realize that she had tried GHB, a new drug her friends offered her that they said would make her feel more alive. Instead, she felt like she had died and landed here, somewhere between consciousness and wanting to die, begging to die.

The cab ride to her apartment was a blur. Meshing cars, swallowed screams, blurred teary-eyed vision. Her shower and all the soap in the world could not clean her the way she needed, and she cried herself to sleep. Sonia vowed that she would clean herself up for good. This was not the woman she wanted to be.

When she woke the next day, she called off work and went directly to an out-patient drug counselor. Reliving the experience from the night before took Sonia to memories of many sordid nights in the past. 'Was I raped—raped?!—before and just couldn't call a spade a spade? What else had happened to me? During those nights of parties, drugs, and lost inhibitions. How far had I let myself float away?'

Drugs, sex, and rock and roll was more than a saying for Sonia, it was her mantra. She grew up thinking this was the life. Hanging out with friends, club hopping, drugs and sex. The doctor listened as Sonia spoke of wanting a change, and needing something more from her life. He listened intently and then suggested a few alternatives for her sobriety. Sonia felt calm and knew this was the only way for her to get the help she needed.

The next few weeks were very hard for her, and she promised to stay clear of Frederic and her other friends who used. She knew it would hurt, but nothing like the reality that she may have been raped, or worst, gave away herself like a child carelessly giving away their innocence.

She went to Narcotics Anonymous meetings and heard stories that trumped hers, making her even more fearful of what doing drugs again could lead to for her future. Maybe, she should count her blessings she thought, as people spoke of the most dire straits she had ever heard. All she could think about was her friends, the old ones who she would hopefully never have to hear going through stories like she was hearing at these meetings. Looking at the faces of people who looked twice her age, but were younger, aging due to the excess of drug use and alcohol abuse. Every night she would count her blessings and pray for brighter days and to regain her consciousness and her life.

She imagined meeting Frederic the morning she last saw him as an opportunity to help him, somehow share some of her newfound wisdom and maybe even get him to come to a meeting. But, walking away from the café that sunny morning, she had to accept that she might never see him again. For Sonia, that was the day Frederic had died.

Sonia stood in the cool night's air as her phone rang to Fredric's mother. Each drag from her cigarette her salvation as she meandered through her brain, what on earth to say to this poor woman. Was Fred gonna be okay? It's like you forget people have parents when you're partying all the time and hanging out. Until moments like this when someone has to call the parents and let them know what happened to their child.

"Hello." Ms. Leon's voice heavy and full of sleep.

"I'm sorry to call you at this hour; it's about Frederic, Ms. Leon."

The silence on the other end of the phone was deafening,

Sonia hung the phone, more tears streaming down her cheeks, but this time she felt a little bit better. Definitely proud of herself for being sober and having the strength to be the responsible person out of the group. She imagined what she would have said if she had a child and had been receiving this phone call at this hour in the morning. She couldn't believe how silent Frederic's mother was during their conversation. She had met his mother only once before but remembered the woman being the life of the party. Such a beautiful woman she had thought that first time they met, and now she imagined her booking a flight from Chicago to California, getting dressed, calling a taxi to take her to the airport. She saw this woman becoming frail, as the seconds passed by her without the ability to do anything. Just wait and sit, and sit some more.

William had walked back into the waiting room when Sonia got on the phone and Sonia was happy that he did.

She had no clue how much Frederic's mother knew of William and his relationship with her son. She pulled out another cigarette and lit it, in her head repeating the Serenity prayer over and over again.

God grant me the serenity to accept the things I cannot change, the courage to change the things I can, and the wisdom to know the difference.

drink_#10

BRYAN

When Bryan screamed in the waiting room of the
emergency room he felt a sense of himself for the first time
in awhile. He was finding his voice. Something that he lost
a long time ago, a space and time when he was too innocent
to know that he was giving it away, letting something
precious go forever. Luckily not forever, he thought to
himself. He had found his voice again. Not by writing in
his journal like everyone used to tell him to do. Or writing
poems like Frederic suggested, but by being hurt again by
someone he had loved. Hurt to a point where he thought he
might not come back.

I feel like I don't know anything at all. It's like waking up
one day and someone telling you that the day was not
actually the day, the day has been and always will be night.
Then that must mean that I've been in the dark when I
thought it was light. Like I thought Frederic and I had a real
thing, a love affair that had been held back for so long but
now was coming out into the light, or dark. Now, it is night.
And I am the one alone, confused and pissed the fuck off.
He made me believe that he was getting better - at least that

he was in love with me. I can't say that I was so concerned with him being with anyone but me. Maybe I was just too gullible.

I am still sitting in this hospital with Sonia and with William. No word on Frederic yet, still in critical condition, still no words or mental movement; he is in a coma. I've considered leaving here three times. But when Sonia described Frederic's mother as silent and stoic, as if a calm other worldliness came over her, I couldn't move. But mostly Sonia said that she was non-existent, like she knew something that we didn't, like she had been waiting for this phone call for a long time, and now that the call was finally upon her she did not have the words, or the tears, or anything. She was silent, like the dawn, the dew landing on the tip of grace – positioned firmly in midair.

I had only met his mother once, and she was the opposite of silent; she was full of life, and she was always staring at Frederic, as if any moment would be her last. I didn't realize that until just now. Something about the way she stared at him intrigued me then, but now that he might die, I am closer to understanding his mother's face and her eyes locked on her only child.

Tears rushed again from my eyes as I sat in my chair pretending to be able to feel the silent pain that she must be feeling. Sonia and William helped each other cope. They have been smoking cigarettes as if their lives depended on it. All the while we won't speak to each other at all; we sit in silence rummaging through our own thoughts and memories of our individual relationships with Frederic. I guess we were all thinking of his poor mother and whether or not he will make it. And, somewhat selfishly, if we will survive if he doesn't.

I've felt this angry before.

Maybe it was the time when my mother left for the Phillipines, leaving me alone with my father. He was so abusive to me and my brother. Everything I did was too sensitive, or not good enough. Every time he saw me it seemed like I reminded him of something he hated inside.

Or maybe the anger was familiar to when I lost my little brother. It seems like one catastrophe after the other popped into my mind. Just thinking of Frederic has me longing for my mother again. Wishing I could hug my brother just once more.

Looking through the magazines on the table, searching for my brother's nose, or his eyes, like flashlights brightening every moment, every darkness. I hold my own hand remembering Frederic's touch. Will that be the last time? The last time we made love or the last time I hear his silly laugh. Is it over? Was he leaving me for William? Was this trip going to be our last time as us? Like everything that leaves, I have to remain strong, standing and pretending like everything is together. Too many times I had to wear the mask, the shielding of the real me, the emotional cover-up. My brain is running toward every possible exit strategy for me right now. Too many questions and too much uncertainty, I can't do it anymore.

I feel my body move before I hear them asking me where I am going. I feel the tears rushing down my face as the hospital becomes further and further away in the rearview mirror. All I can hear is the engine humming as trees pass as fast as the memories of Frederic. I am leaving this time. You can have him William. I can't wait here to find out anymore, to hear that he is dead, or that he wants William, or that he still wants me. How can I trust him? Or myself?

My mother's face is etched into my thoughts, like hieroglyphics, cultural reminders, a sketch of where we begin and ultimately end. We use to talk about going to see the pyramids and ruins of the world to find our unique sketches, our stories. But she left before we could take that trip together. She walked out the door carrying only one bag, and continued out into the parked taxi waiting for her outside our house. I didn't know exactly where she was going, but I felt in my heart that she was going for good. Leaving me and never coming back ever again. Everyone seemed to always leave before they were supposed to.

I don't know if I am pissed because Frederic left me or because I have been hiding behind him and everything else for that matter, avoiding my own shit. When he came back, it felt like the world had eased my own thoughts of suicide and craziness. I guess I never dealt with my mother leaving or my brother's death, or my fucking father. I only deal with dick it seems, and of course work. I like to get buried in it. Dick and work. Just blind myself to everything else that is so blinding. Bind myself to a man or paycheck, and keep smiling Bryan - keep everyone else feeling better, somehow I'll feel good too. Keep walking away from the light in order to know the darkness, I guess. But, now I don't know a damn thing anymore. If I don't have Frederic, I ain't got nothing.

Frederic's mother's face appears as the dark night pulls me in. Enter mother; exit lover. Images of my own mother's face return and lastly my brother's before I hear myself scream again. I scream my brother's name, 'Tommie,' and my heart begins to beat faster than the speedometer. They all seem to be telling me something. I don't want to hear it, and I scream again, like in the hospital but this time I can't stop. I drive without a care, 100 mph, 140 mph. The car feels like me, angry but destined to leave this time, wanting to move faster away from everything. Wanting to get the fuck out of here. To get away, to leave, to be in that bed with Frederic, and to die. To lay with Frederic, dying.

'But dad, I didn't do anything.' His angry fist lands on my temple, and I feel like I'm going to throw up, or pass out.

'What are you doing in here then? Who are these men in these pictures? Why are your pants down to your knees? Bryan, what's going on?' His eyes are red like fire. His voice always harder than his punches, always hard, never loving, never willing to know me for myself. He grabs me like a pile of dirty clothes and slams my body into the ground. I hurriedly pull my pants up reaching for the pictures. His fists, rapid and profound, hit me everywhere I try to block. When I see the blood from my nose I cry louder for help. But, there is no one. There is never anyone to help. He just stands over me looking down like the next punch would kill me.

'I hate you. If this is who you are going to be, then I want nothing to do with you. You are a disgrace.' The door slams, and I breathe a breath of calm. I pick up all of my pictures, and clean my room.

I know he is going to his car. I hear the engine fire up. I know he is going to drink himself into a daze and then come back home. He is going to knock on my door, ever so faint, and then walk in. He is going to grab me from under my sheets and hold me in his arms, like he does all the time. Then he is going to fall asleep. He will not let me go until he wakes up. I know better than to move. The whole time I pretend I'm sleep. The whole time I am wishing he would be like this when he is sober. This is the pattern. This is my life with my father.

In the morning when I wake up, he is gone. Sometimes I think I get caught doing things he doesn't like on purpose so that he can beat me and then return home to apologize. You know what they say about arguments: the best part is when you make up. I wait for his return when we have arguments. Usually, I sit in my underwear with the lights off until I hear the car pull up and his feet on the staircase. I lie down under the sheets, and wait. This is the only time he ever touches me like a father, or like a human. He holds me so close to him I can smell every drink he had that night. My father the drunk, the abusive man, the only man I think I ever will love. The only man I think ever loved me enough to hurt me. And the only man who ever apologized. I know this is a sick reality, but it's all I got with him. His angry fists and his strong, powerful arms that hold me seem to be all we got together. This is the only way that my father knows how to love me. I accept it, and sometimes miss him terribly.

The thought crosses my mind of death and of Frederic dying. I hear the shrill of the tires before I notice the car turning around. I drive as fast as I can back to the hospital. I'm not losing Frederic like this - I refuse to let him leave

me. Never will Frederic leave me; he told me that, and I
still believe him.

_____

drink #11 JON

You know how god gives you only enough for you to handle? I always would hear people say that. I'm not deeply religious. I don't even believe in God, per se. I believe in a higher power, and I know it exists. Maybe it was when I lost my mother and found something bigger than myself in the process. I think it was then that I knew there was something greater than me out there. It would have to be right? How could a child be responsible for burying their mother? The only thing that got me through those times was the reality that life had to be about something else. Life was ultimately about death. Which meant that everything I ever did and would do would lead me to death as well.

Most of the time Frederic was the life of the party, so when I heard that he was lying in a hospital, and in a coma on a Saturday night, I knew the end was near. No way Frederic would be anywhere but a party on the weekends, and I think that is a direct quote from him. We had our good times and we had our bad, but getting the call from Sonia scared the hell out of me. I think at the time she called, I could have cared less what was going on with him. Of course, that was because what I thought was going on had nothing to do with blood or hospitals.

Sometimes humans get so angry that we don't ever want, for the time being, to see the person who made us angry again. Of course we don't mean that, but what we do mean is that we want a space created where we can begin to try and love that person again, at least miss their companionship enough to let the evil that men do erase and fall back into the crevices of the past. At least, that is what I had hoped for Frederic and I. As far as I was concerned, Frederic was dead, and I didn't want to see him until I resurrected him again as someone I wanted in my life. That is where he and I were very similar; we were able to rid our mind of people who took too much space and did not add anything special to our lives. But, eventually, the people we said we would never again speak to were hanging out with us soon enough.

That night Frederic came and got his bags from my apartment was one of those cold ass San Francisco nights. The wind from the bay, and the fact that it never gets too hot here, created this sense of winter that just shouldn't be experienced in the fall. The cold and bitter way I was feeling toward this asshole did not help me feel any warmth. It was like he was already becoming a stranger to me, as I waited for him each night to come back to the apartment. I knew Frederic partied, and I wanted to party with him, you know, just a little before the engagement party. I mean damn, I thought he was coming back here for a job and might need to rest and hang out with his friend. Maybe that is what made me so angry after all of these years being in his life, he still treated me like I was a second or third world citizen in his world. See, Frederic was like the mayor. He was like the Daley's of Chicago, loved by many and hated by equally as many—or more. I think it was his personality and his natural way with people. And his big fucking mouth. He would talk you down and up on any conversation, and have the person in the bar who hated him the most at the onset of the evening buying him rounds of drinks toward the end of the night.

Charming to say the least, good looking, and smart as a bonus, Frederic was everyone's best friend, but no one's real friend when it came down to it. It didn't matter anyway; most people don't want much from you but a good time and to feel special sometimes. And Frederic was great at giving a good time, as well as other things, and

eventually feeling special was part of the deal. He even
made you feel good when you paid for his drinks, or his
food, or his rent. He had this crazy charm that everyone,
and I mean everyone, wanted to be under. I cannot and will
not tell you how many straight men he slept with, for
starters, because he told me never to tell anyone, and
second, I would have to tell on myself too.

I know. It sounds weird, we were like brothers, but actually
more like whatever we wanted to be. He gave me a sense of
myself outside of what everyone else told me to be. He
made me feel beautiful, wanted, welcomed, and free. He
had this sense of talking to you where you felt like you
were the only person in the world, and these words were
carved out of time to help you make more sense of
everything. Give you some perspective from the gods, or
from somewhere deep inside that you would have never
tapped into without him. I think that's why so many people
gave him everything, and he always wanted to be
everything for everyone, except himself. They say people
who like to help do so, so they can help someone—cause
lord knows they can't help themselves. Look at me talking
like he's not here anymore. I know he is going to make it
through this, he always does, just like one of those comic

book characters we used to be when we was younger. Sometimes I still wish I had magic powers.

My engagement party was not as fun as I had hoped it would be. Everyone there was kind of waiting on Frederic. That was a little strange for me, you know being the man of the evening, at least in my own head. But, I understood. Shit, I was waiting for Frederic too. Knowing in my heart he wasn't coming but hoping somewhere in this same heart that he would show up and save my boring party.

Been sitting here with this cell phone in my hand, toying with the idea that I need to call his mother or call Sonia back. Instead I dial Frederic's phone and leave him a message. I think that's what makes me know that he is going to be fine. I hear him laughing with me as I tell my stale jokes. I see his eyes, all big, and sweet, and welcoming, staring off into the distance listening to my attempt at a joke but still laughing with me. The next phone I call is Frederic's mother, but it just goes to voicemail. Her voice a ball of energy and charisma, but I can't meet the energy and just hang up the phone. I don't think I'm going to that hospital, but I can't see how I couldn't. 'Damn it', I think to myself, and realize that tears start forming in my eyes. Maybe, I think, I will go.

Before I know it I am in my car and driving North toward Calistoga. Something inside of me tells me that I need to get to him as soon as possible. I don't think he is going to die, but I don't know what to think.

EPILOGUE

"If we know ourselves, do we know our children? Are they, indeed, extensions of us? Or separate people? Independent thinkers who were somehow created by us, out of our image? Am I god?

Raising Frederic was a pleasure of mine. He was *my* son. You know, I made him all by myself. Myself and god. I would say that he was my jesus, and I was like mary; that Fredric was immaculately conceived. Since the father was a ghost, ha ha, I mean he was nowhere to be found, so I made it up that he was sent by god to me.

And now god has taken him away.

Ain't…there is nothing like a mother burying her son, I'll tell ya that. And now to know all of the pain my poor baby was going through. And to think I blamed some of you for his pain. *Blamed you.* When that pain was his and his alone. I mean I have blamed myself something wicked. And sometimes I still think, what if I would have done this that way, and what if I sent him to live with his grandparents or something, anything else. But, I know you can't think like that. You can't get back tomorrow no matter how far you reach out for it. It's gone, forever out of reach.

Gone like my baby. Not all the way gone, we all got the memories, right? I know some of you out there got some stories to tell me about my boy. And I want to hear them too. Don't go worrying about me, I got my own stories to rival the mischief I know my boy was out here doing. But, I still want to know. Because, I don't judge him or you. You gotta live your life, some way. Any way that makes you happy, huh? I mean I have. I had my son and never looked back for ghosts. Ain't gonna look back now either. I'ma be like my son and be a badass, let the wind kiss my ass as I move through this world fearlessly, boundless. I'ma get in more trouble and learn more lessons. But, mainly I'ma walk on that side of life my son walked on.

He was looking for love.

Always looking for the fulfillment of love. Whether it was in the arms of this man or that woman, or taking this drug and working in god knows where, my son was on a quest for love.

Especially, in that school that day. I think he lived and died that day. Those of you who knew my son, I mean really knew him, know that he was a fighter. But, that fight knocked it out of him. Took the wind out of him ya know.

But, like I said we ain't…we're not here to lay any blame on nobody now. We here to celebrate that boy Frederic Leon. My boy. Something of a somebody.
He will be missed.
Always missed.
And always free.
My boy lived free, and my boy died free.
Y'all tell his story. Tell them about that black boy who loved him some of life.
Loved him some men, and some beautiful women.
He was in love with love.

And I will always love him. Always."

Ms. Leon walked from the pulpit to her seat in the front row of the huge church. Every row was full, from young folks to older family friends.

She sat down next to her brother. Jon, Sonia, William and Bryan sat along side her with the rest of Frederic's family.

When the Preacher asked everyone to lower their heads in prayer, Ms. Leon stood up and quietly walked over and kissed Jon, Sonia, William and Bryan on the cheek, before she walked stoic out of the church doors. Her brother walking closely behind her every step, as the church doors open and close behind them.

Angels BY FREDERIC LEON, age 10

who knows if i'll live forever?
who knows if and when i'll ever die?
i don't think i want to know those things
i would rather know the angels.
the angels above and the angels
below.
id rather know those kinds of things.

Dedicated to all the writers and all the stories....
and of course Darlene Peebles, my mother, and always, Levonia Peebles.

ANTHONY DWIGHT PEEBLES (Khalil Anthony)
Photo by HALDUN MORGAN

Khalil Anthony is an Artist-Educator, working within varying mediums and media. His work investigates the relationships between the spirit and space, the black body, sexuality, and society, and the urban experience. Weaving together these artistic intentions through dance and movement, writing, painting, education, and song, his work speaks to a diverse audience and to varying communities.

Originally from Chicago, Illinois and currently living in New York City, this celebrated educator, dancer and artist has taught and performed in the UK, Amsterdam, Paris, Venezuela, Brazil, Mexico, Guatemala, and throughout the continental US. His performance and arts-education work stem from a belief and commitment in the knowledge that all human beings, and especially young people, have a voice.

Frederic Leon is his first novel. www.khalilanthony.com

Made in the USA
Monee, IL
11 December 2023

47896865R10135